SURVEYOR

Also by G. W. Hawkes

Semaphore
Spies in the Blue Smoke
Playing Out of the Deep Woods

SURVEYOR

G . W . HAWKES

MacMurray & Beck
Denver

ABR- 9658

Acknowledgments are due and are gratefully made to the following:
The passage quoted on page ix is from "Desert Places," Robert Frost,
Robert Frost Poetry and Prose, edited by Edward Connery Lathem and Lawrance
Thompson (New York: Holt, Rinehart and Winston, 1972).

"Surveyor," a short story taken from this manuscript,
was published in *Spies in the Blue Smoke*
(University of Missouri Press, 1992).

Printed and bound in the United States of America

1   2   3   4   5   6   7   8   9   10

Library of Congress Cataloging-in-Publication Data
Hawkes, G. W., 1953–
Surveyor : a novel / by G. W. Hawkes.
p.   cm.
ISBN 1-878448-81-1
I. Title.
PS3558.A818S87 1998
813'.54—dc21   97-47036
CIP

MacMurray & Beck Fiction: General Editor, Greg Michalson
Surveyor cover design by Laurie Dolphin,
cover photograph by Michel Madie,
interior design by Stacia Schaefer.
The text was set in Weiss by Chris Davis, Mulberry Tree Enterprises.

JUN 2 4 1998

this and all others
for Kay

Three people, a long time ago, helped with this manuscript: Larry Woiwode, John Vernon, and Susan Strehle

They cannot scare me with their empty spaces
Between stars—on stars where no human race is.
I have it in me so much nearer home
To scare myself with my own desert places.

Robert Frost

1

John thumped a paper bag down on the table and lifted out four stacks of bills, banded fifties and hundreds. He pulled out four more. "I want an end to debt," he said.

"How much have you got there?"

"My half of things. Two hundred and some-odd thousand."

"That should do it, John, considering we don't owe anybody anything."

"I owe you," he said. "I want to get square."

I kept silent as he emptied the bag, piling a hundred and four green bricks into a pyramid, and then lowered himself slowly into a straightbacked chair. He winced as his new leg pinched.

"It still hurts?"

"They said it would." He pushed his knee flat until the leg was straight. He tapped the gray plastic with his fingernail, loosing the sound a ring makes striking something hollow. "Take what's yours," he said, waving at the money.

I pulled out the chair across from him, resting my hands on the table. The New Mexico morning fell on them in soft, butter-colored triangles. "What could you possibly owe me?"

"Let's start with the gin score. It's the largest."

The game is decades old. In our deliberate incarceration we've run up some enormous debts to each other, but only because games need rules.

I told him that. "It isn't fair to you," I said. "The game's perpetual. And you're way behind."

"Humor me."

I've watched John more than once build his own face from clay, fashioning the whole head, even the bald spot at his crown and the scar behind his left ear, and then when the sculpture hardened, drop a rock on it. I don't like to admit it, but there are parts of John, still, that I can't guess at.

"Have I done something?"

He, too, looked at the light on my hands. It was one of those rare, almost conjugal moments in this life of near celibacy. "No, Paul." He rubbed his leg, as if easing a real cramp, and then rubbed his eyes. "I just want to settle up."

"I'll wipe it out."

"I'll pay it."

"It's scorekeeping; it's not meant to be paid."

"How much?"

I retrieved the scoresheet from under the cards on the bookcase and had to squint. "Seventeen hundred and forty-two dollars and thirty-nine cents."

He pulled a pen from his shirt pocket and dug in his wallet until he found a folded square of paper—the bank receipt—and asked me the number again and wrote it down. "Chess?"

"I owe you eighty bucks."

He started another column. "Cribbage?"

"You're ahead twenty-seven games," I said. I watched him cross out the eighty and write three hundred fifty in his loose, spidery hand.

"Guesses?"

In this mood there's no reasoning with him. "I'll get the books." I turned toward the door, turned back. "This will take some time. You don't have a plane to catch or anything?"

"I'm not in the mood for funny, Paul."

"I see you're not."

Our guesses are in our surveying logs. In the early days we'd guessed about everything: spoor we'd find, sediments we were standing on, geologic time, the names of the constellations and their number (eighty-eight, the same as a piano's keys), next week's temperature, last year's rainfall, anything, and in one drunken moment years later, we'd fixed a hundred-dollar price tag on each. The money meant nothing between us; the Foundation funds us in perpetuity, and the work we do somehow funds the Foundation.

These guesses, over the years, have become whatever truth we've found, whatever facts we have in our lives, as we've given up trying to do the job right. We add mesas and draws and sometimes whole mountain ranges, and we change the courses of rivers. It doesn't much matter to us anymore where we put things. It did at first, when we were new out of college with some military discipline still in us, hired by Arlyle to survey this place; then, we drew each contour carefully, and John molded the desert's likeness in clay. But now, after nearly thirty years, we change this landscape to suit ourselves.

I carried in the first—that is, last—of the boxes of log-books and set it on the table next to the money.

John pulled out a handful of the narrow, spiral-backed notebooks we've begun to use and opened the first of them. "Get the calculator, will you? It's on top of the fridge."

I unfolded the desert, perforated at the side. It's an archaeology of sorts. In our notebooks are the habits and the leavings of the mountain lion and the skeletons of the mule deer and the camouflage and speed of the long-eared hares, the bristles of burros and wild horses, local recipes for alcohol that you can squeeze from juniper and cactus, drawings of rare trees, diagrams like you'd find on the floor of an Arthur Murray dance studio of the crablike steps of the large black scorpion that hides in roots of rocks and curls around tent pegs at night for heat, and the smaller, glasslike, nearly invisible cousin that we call ventana, window, everything we could find out about the brown tarantula and the larger, red-striped one, the tiny brown recluse migrating north from Mexico, the diamondback rattlesnake, and the occasional lost gila monster. Half a billion insects live here with us: hated mosquitoes and horseflies, grasshoppers in biblical multitudes, dragonflies that appear out of nowhere with the spring rains, crickets, and larger, luminous, iridescent-backed beetles whose clacking wings sound like castanets. We've sketched mice and prairie-dog holes and crows and magpies and the ostrichlike roadrunner (I see a note here, in the margin: *struthious*), and hawks—not as often now—that circle in the high thermals, and cliff-dwelling swallows, and owls.

We've even plotted human migrations. In this part of New Mexico, where the corners of four states collide, slip, and collide again, there are three horse ranchers, two towns, and any number of prospectors—young, old, with families and without—whom we suffer to pass through our desert like gypsies, hunting gold, silver, bauxite, uranium. The military not too many miles away has burrowed under the Sangre de Cristo Mountains and laid their atomics down deep holes, and we know that the desert under us is hollow and glass-hearted.

Surveyors, too, have stumped through every few years, USGS types, and we entertain them for a few days as brothers should, and we show them our good set of books: the early clay scale maps we made that rightly capture the external geometry of this place. All of this, in one way or another, is chronicled in our guesses.

I flipped a page, saw a note: 29.92S. We've come to trust, after years of guessing, the barometer John carries in his missing leg: a ghostly weather needle accurate to the hundredth of an inch.

"This is wrong," I said, after I'd looked through half a log. On one recent page I saw that John had incorrectly guessed the number of stars in the Pleiades (seeing six and guessing ten) while I had figured a small mesa to be exactly thirty-two hundred and twenty-five feet above sea level. "We wouldn't have made these bets if we had to pay off."

"There's always a reckoning," John said.

"What's bothering you?"

He got up heavily and rapped the table once with one huge hand and then turned and went out. The screen door banged and I heard his iambic soundprint on the porch— something I can't get used to: the new, hydraulic ta-*dum* of John walking instead of the nearly noiseless swinging of his rubber-tipped crutches—and then he left the porch and was off into the desert. I stood at the door and watched him go.

Sparrow-sized butterflies tumbled about in my solar plexus. John acted like this when he was confused, when confronted by cosmic plans, when he was facing God or UFOs or Arlyle.

John met Arlyle only once, three decades ago. We'd often wonder, when we'd nothing else to do, whether he's still living and whether he still runs things. All of the Foundation's correspondence to us (mostly our paychecks) has strangers' names scrawled in undecipherable signatures above still stranger titles, but in the days of the Foundation's beginnings, in the middle of Eisenhower's administration, there was only Arlyle.

John had a degree in history with a minor in art. I'd done my work in engineering. We'd been together since Korea, when through no fault of my own I found myself driving an ambulance and loading him as cargo. We were discharged a month apart from the same hospital, enrolled in the same college, rented a house with the money we drew from the GI Bill and the boarders we took in—mostly other older students like ourselves—graduated finally, and answered the Foundation's advertisement in the *Washington Post*'s classifieds that said, in effect, they'd hire anybody. The country was like that, then.

We rode the bus down from Boston to West Hewing, Maryland, where the Foundation had its offices in the basement of an abandoned library, but was moving. We met a couple of sweating men on the stairs and had to back up and wait outside while they dragged up a filing cabinet.

"I'd take the drawers out first," John said to nobody.

I'd grown used to this. Just the two of us were standing on the steps in a cold wind, and John could have been talking to me, but of course he wasn't.

I answered him anyway. "You've got a college education." We believed, then, that an education set us apart, that those without it would stand off to the side like Neanderthals and watch history go on without them. He

leaned into the wind with his hands in his pockets and did-
n't say anything else. When the cabinet got to the top of
the stairs we went back in, and down, and found Arlyle.

He looked thirty or so, not much older than we, and
even so young he was going bald. He was clean-shaven,
dressed expensively in a gray chalkstripe banker's suit, and
tall enough to hitch himself up without any effort to a sitting position on an upended desk. There was that and a
filing cabinet in the room—brother to the one bumping
around upstairs—and three large open cardboard boxes of
books and papers. Arlyle looked for John's left leg without
embarrassment, then seemed to weigh the crutches.

"Mer*line* and Swope?"

John smiled, but I answered phonetically, "Merlin,"
and raised my hand, still in the classroom. "And Sope. The
e's silent in my name; the u's silent in his."

He peered at us. He brought a pair of glasses out of his
vest pocket as a man would a watch and held them by an
earpiece.

John spun around on his crutches in a little one-
footed, five-step shuffle that he used to perform for people
who doubted his agility.

"Paul," I said before Arlyle took the bait. "And John."

The moving men came back down for the desk. Arlyle
pointed instead to the filing cabinet. The laborers ignored
him, hefted a box apiece, and went out.

Arlyle reached with his other hand into the breast
pocket of his suit jacket, where the handkerchief goes, as

if reaching for a cigarette or a pencil, but brought his hand out empty. "I need two men to go to New Mexico for a while."

"To do what?" John asked.

"Look at the land." He gave John a long, myopic stare, and then shifted back to me. Most people do. John's eyes are such a pale green they're disturbing. And there's that— or rather, there isn't that—missing leg.

"I have a history degree," John said. His belligerence was a warning to me. I looked at Arlyle while Arlyle looked at John, but I couldn't see in him what John evidently saw.

"You've studied art," Arlyle said.

"Sculpture."

"Sculpture," Arlyle agreed. "You sculpt."

It sounds dirty to me, even after all these years. It's the sort of thing you'd say under your breath at a cocktail party ("That's John: he sculpts"), but we don't go to many cocktail parties. He's not a hammer-and-chisel sort of sculptor; he collects things and makes piles of them, and of course he does what he has to in order to make his maps.

"You need a sculptor?" John asked.

Arlyle nodded.

"In the desert?"

"Yes."

John shrugged and in the same motion shoved his hands back into his pockets. That's a strange sight: the two wooden legs of his crutches, the good muscle-and-bone one, and his hands in his pockets. A human tripod. He leaned against the wall, as a kangaroo might if it had a broken tail. Arlyle turned back to me. The movers came back down and walked the filing cabinet across the floor, tilted it, and began to push it up the stairs.

"I'd take the drawers out," John said.

Arlyle frowned. "And you're an engineer," he said to me.

I nodded.

"You said in your letter that you've done some surveying."

"Not a lot of it. In the army."

"I need a cartographer."

"I can make maps."

"I need detailed maps." Impossibly, he stressed neither syllable in *detailed*.

I thought about that while I answered. "That's a matter of scale."

"All right, then," he said, and jumped down. "You're hired. Both of you."

John and I glanced at each other but passed no messages.

"If you want the jobs," Arlyle added.

I flicked another look at John, but he wasn't having any. He was staring at the bare wall behind Arlyle.

"Seven thousand a year each," Arlyle said. He put his glasses on and looked John's way, then mine. "And all expenses, of course." He took another quick look at John, guessing where the decision would come from. "Food and clothes and extras, too."

"Let me get this straight," I said. "You want me to make detailed maps of New Mexico?"

"Actually," he said, smiling, "only a small part of it. And I want you to survey the ground. I want *him* to make the maps."

"You want me to sculpt them," John said.

"Exactly."

"We'd like to talk this over," I said.

"All right."

John pivoted to lead me out. He pivoted back. "Just what is it that your Foundation does, Mr. Arlyle?"

"We'll just have to wait and see," he said, and John and I took that to mean *you'll* have to wait and see, but I think now that he meant exactly what he said.

We passed the men again on the stairs, and all of us flattened against the wall to get by. John crabbed up gracefully on his crutches, even though pressed against the wall like the rest of us.

I looked out the screen door thirty years later and watched him make his way down the slope, tied to that new machinery that hurt him. That wasn't Arlyle's doing, or God's either. It wasn't the leg, but there was a connection—something, some small mannerism or piece of conversation—that I was missing; something John had just done, just said, that had called up that first meeting with

Arlyle, and I couldn't figure it. I turned away from the door and got a beer from the fridge and thought about it.

We'd left Arlyle and ordered coffee at a diner. We had two hours before the bus left for Boston.

"You don't want to do it," I said to John when the coffee came.

"That's a queer guy." He spread his fingers in a vee, wanting a cigarette. I gave him one and reached over to light it. Then I lit one for myself. "The job's queer, too," he said.

"What difference does that make?" I was surprised at him, more surprised, even, than I was that anybody wanted to hire both of us.

John blew smoke out his nose like a horse will on a cold morning. I've never learned the knack of blowing smoke through my nose while talking; the air passages in John's head must be different from mine. I'd missed what he'd said, watching the smoke.

"What?"

"What do you think he's up to?"

I shrugged. It didn't matter.

"And another thing," he said, but he only drank his coffee.

"And another thing, what?" I asked after a time.

"That Foundation. It's one man, and maybe some money."

"So?"

"And another thing."

I waited.

"New Mexico."

"Yeah?"

"Where the hell is that?"

"Near Texas," I said.

"There's nothing near Texas."

"The Gulf is."

He looked into his hand, as if he'd find a map there. "How long do you think it'll take to map New Mexico? *Part* of New Mexico," he said, correcting himself.

"Have you got somewhere else to go?"

He shook his head.

"Somewhere you have to be in two years that I don't know about?"

He shook his head again, not answering the questions but trying to stop them, and I should have known by then that that's what it was.

"You don't like deserts?"

"All right!" He held up both hands to apologize. "All right," he said more quietly. "You don't feel it."

"Feel what?"

"New Mexico might be like Korea."

"Rocky? Cold?"

He leaned his elbows on the table and flexed his biceps. The flexing was unconscious with him, but it intimidated everybody, even me. It's what he did in those days before he started arguments. "Didn't you know the day you walked ashore that Korea was the wrong place to be?"

I said no.

"You really didn't?"

I shook my head.

"You were a grunt, just like me," he said accusingly. "Before they made you a meatwagon driver."

"*That* was the dangerous part. If I'd stayed a grunt I would have been okay."

He ignored me. "Korea was full of everybody but Koreans."

"Well—"

"The whole world crowded their armies in there."

"Well—"

"It got so you had to look at their badges before you could shoot somebody."

"Yeah, but—"

"And it's going to be the same in New Mexico."

"We're going to shoot somebody?"

He gave me a look. "It's a wrong place," he said. "For me."

"Then we don't go."

He stared into the bottom of his empty coffee cup. "Just like that?"

"Just like that."

We did go, of course. Here we are.

I got up and went to the door again. I hadn't understood all those years ago what he'd been saying. I'd thought he'd meant New Mexico and Korea were tangled up in a premonition or something, that John was afraid he'd lose another leg. Who could have known, then, that he'd find one? But it wasn't that; it never had been. I know now it was not wanting to ever again be a stranger to a place, to come without an invitation. And all of it had something to do, now, with zeroing out these silly bets.

I stared until I found one black dot moving that might be John. The desert was too full to be sure. And we hadn't invited any of them.

This is an arid, sandscrubbed, hateful land, as barren as Mars. Even the Indians don't want it. It's altogether beautiful, but we don't own it anymore. Those few we've come to accept as belonging here, like Wilkens, who raises quarterhorses, or Jamieson, who for years has been building a huge antenna out of sand in order to talk to the stars, seem strangers now as well as strange, and threatening. The delicate ratio of human to empty square mile has crossed an invisible threshold and like cargo shifting in a poorly loaded freighter promises only disaster. This must be what John sees.

It was that box of our early logs and the smell of old paper and dusty cardboard that triggered that thirty-year-old memory of Arlyle among his boxes, but it's been my experience that old memories resurrected from the grave demand a life of their own, precipitate events, in fact, in some mysterious fashion, as if the universe runs not on physical laws but by coincidence: glittering triangles of happenstance that fall jumbled across each other like broken glass panes in a kaleidoscope. It was this revelation that caused me to tell John, when he returned that evening, that Arlyle was coming.

"What? When?"

"Soon." He had to be, didn't he?

"Why?"

"I don't know."

It's a measure of our friendship that John never asked to see the letter or wonder how I knew. He would have gotten from me quickly that it was my own supposition, based on nothing but a recollection and perhaps a desire. And if I'd asked myself why I wanted to see Arlyle again, I probably couldn't have answered, then, that I wanted him to return the desert to its rightful owners. It's odd that I would think he could.

John dropped down on to the sofa. His pain was apparent in the dark, twisting veins across the backs of his huge hands. I counted his heartbeat in them.

"Did you finish the guesses?"

"Nope. And I'm not going to," I said, deciding as I said it not to. "You can look those figures up for yourself if you want them."

He threw a long look at me, but I've learned to meet those eyes, and he finally gave up and dragged his hands from the back of the sofa and down into his lap. "How about buying an old man a beer?"

When I'd brought him one, he said, "The Dinosaur Men have found something new. They have a whole side of Gonzalitos opened up and are raking bones out of it like strips of coal."

"What are they this time?"

He shrugged, upended the beer can, and then shook it at me, rattling the pop top that I drop in it out of habit. I got him another.

"I figured Arlyle must be dead by now," he said.

"Me too." I looked around the room as if I'd find in one of the corners an answer for the question that had to be coming, but wasn't.

"The girl's still hammering away."

"She'd better hurry." It was a small miracle that an early storm hadn't already washed through that gully.

"I told her that," he said. "She's enlisted me."

"Is that where you've been?"

"I told her I'd trade my labor for her lumber."

Fear pinged in my chest like a muscle coming loose, but I worked up a smile and said, "We've got enough wood for the stove."

"I know."

"Gonna build mousetraps?"

"Boxes, Paul." He sighed and pushed himself to his feet.

I saw a formal occasion coming. "Sit down," I said. "You're beat."

He stood anyway. "I'm going to build boxes for my sculptures. For most of the maps. For the few paintings I've done." He ran a hand over his short gray hair and tugged at the collar of his flannel shirt. "I'm going to crate them up."

"And then what?"

"And then I'm going to take them into Denver."

"And then what?"

"Show 'em." He said it so softly I had to wait for the words to hit my ear and make themselves comfortable before I understood.

"Show them?" I stood up, too, and looked at the bridge of his nose, which must have made me look crosseyed to him. "On street corners? In alleys? Door to door on your new goddamned leg? 'Excuse me, lady, want to buy a painting? Hey, mister, want to see some art? I got four square feet of desert with some glass stuck in it.' Show them?" I said. "What made you decide that after all this time?"

"Just that, Paul. All this time."

"The crash piece, too?"

"All of it. Except some of the maps."

"When did you decide this?"

"Today."

"You sleep okay last night, John? Are there monsters bumping around under your bed?"

"What's the matter with you?" He sat back down on the sofa, more carefully this time.

"*Me*? What's the matter with *me*?"

"I only want to show my art in Denver."

"And tie up loose ends. And pay off imaginary debts."

"Real debts."

18

"Are you dying?"

"No faster than you are. It's just that I've got to break out of this"—he spread his arms wide enough to take in more than the house—"for a bit."

I had nothing to say to him, so I took a beer and sat out on the porch. The sun was low, almost gone, and the desert was blue. At sunrise the rocks are purple and pink and lavender, the colors you find in the throat of a cat's ear, but as the sun pulls up the colors work themselves into rich creamy yellows, then hard reds, then into the white of noon, a light so hard even the black tar roads and I-25 are white and the flat basin is mirrored. It's blue in the evening, and then purple again, and then black, as if all the day's shadows had collected themselves for the next day's inevitable explosion. We know this place by its colors, and by the hard and soft edges of its light, and that magical moment when the rocks and the sky are the same deep blue is my favorite time.

John opened the screen and stuck his head out, interrupting all of it. "Why does it matter so much to you?" he asked.

I answered as honestly as I could. "I've never thought of your sculptures as art," I said, knowing he'd take it the wrong way.

He banged the door shut.

"But history," I said to nobody. Yours and mine, I didn't even say.

2

The pickup idling woke me in the morning. John was off to help the girl, Caliope.

I poured a cup of coffee from the new pot John had left on the heat and took it out onto the porch, where I sat gingerly—I was naked—in one of the slung canvas chairs. John waved in the near dark, flipped on the truck's lights, and drove down into the wash that's our driveway. The truck bounced, crabbed sideways, and slipped out of sight. The sun hadn't yet climbed over Gonzalitos and the house was still in deep shadow, but the basin below us was in bright morning and newly made. It was like standing in the shrubbery at night and looking into somebody's window.

Our house sits between the two great mesas of Gonzalitos (to the east) and Rayado (to the west) in a high, flat pocket called Horse Thief Gap. The Dinosaur Men would be at work already on Gonzalitos's eastern face, mining black bone from their black shadows, and the girl, too, had the habit of driving her first nail as soon as she had light to see it, but John and I are used to beginning the day late in this last dark corner. It seemed suddenly like hiding, or something more unsavory, and I went in and got dressed.

I knew places John didn't, that he'd never been able to climb to, and I went to one of them, a narrow shelf of rock halfway up Rayado where I had a good view of the girl's emerging town half a mile away. I checked for snakes and scorpions, carefully cleared the rock of small stones with a sweep of my foot, and then sat back on my heels as I'd learned in Korea and put the glasses to my eyes.

The town leaped forward. I could see John plainly. He stood abruptly as my eyes found him, dropped the two-by-four he'd been about to cut, and looked over his shoulder toward the house. The telepathy between us is as clear as radio sometimes. Go back to work, I thought, and as the thought reached him he bent over, squared the board, and began to cut it. I turned the glasses on the girl.

She was dressed, as always, in threadbare cutoff jeans and a dirty white man's singlet that hardly covered her. She turned to say something to John, and I watched her breasts shift under her shirt. I felt welling up in me again the ache that's been dormant for years. It's the reason we've had to stop watching her as I was now.

She'd come to our desert the month before, a month behind the Dinosaur Men. She jumped down from the cab of a lumber truck, almost in our laps as distances in the desert are measured, and I confess we stared. Her nipples under that singlet were like tiny black stones. She ordered two boys to unload the lumber at the edge of a gully, in the mouth of a draw that feeds Miami Lake. We watched until the two boys were finished unloading and had driven off, then we walked down to where she stood among the banded stacks of two-by-fours and sheets of one-eighth-inch plywood squares and told her she'd picked the worst place in the desert to build anything.

"It'll flood," John said, pointing up the draw that drained the tableland and then down below us, where past action had cut a deep arroyo.

She stuck out a pink hand. "Caliope Jones."

John raised a crutch and pointed again at the arroyo. "I've seen a four-foot wall of water come through there." He stabbed his crutch up the draw. "The tableland collects it for a day or so, or an hour or so, depending on the storm, and then lets it all go. Believe me—"

"Caliope."

"Believe me, girl, whatever you build will be washed out."

"Good." She smiled at both of us. Not once did she look at John's missing leg. "From the aerial photos, this looked like the best spot."

"Aerial photos?"

She reached into a knapsack and pulled out a sheaf of them. "I've got this whole corner of the state. Do you want to see it?"

"That's the way we should do it," John said to me.

"It's kind of late now," I said.

"I'm going to build a town," she said as if talking to herself. "A hotel, a gas station, a drugstore, and whatever else I feel like."

"It'll all get washed away."

"I'm counting on it." She gestured vaguely at her gear, leaning in a loose pile against the lumber: a tent and an aluminum tripod, a walking pack, and two large plastic garbage bags tied with plastic fasteners. "I have a video camera," she said. "I want to tape it."

"You're making a movie?"

"It's going to be my dissertation."

"It's science?" John asked.

"My Ph.D.'s in film."

John nodded at her, but I knew he didn't understand any more than I did about the outside world.

She bent over her camera bag to show us, and we both saw that her shorts were worn thin, and we both looked away.

"Is this a good place to camp?" she asked, still bent over.

We both pointed to her left, where a natural rock shelter was cut next to the draw. "I'll show you," John said, and pulled himself that way. She gave me a glorious smile, completely unaware of the effect she was having on two old hermits, a "See you," a wave, and then trotted off after John.

From then on the landscape we chose to recheck had her in it. At a hundred yards we were invisible to her, but she centered the crosshairs like a vision. Who wouldn't have done the same thing? We've learned to think of other things than sex, and then this Californian shows up, built like a boy's Christmas present and nearly naked, and we had no choice. John stopped it, finally.

"This is voyeurism," he said, and took his eye from the transit.

"Yes."

"Especially when we train it on her tent."

"Yes." I pushed him aside and took his place.

"Or the lake."

"That's right, yes." She bathed in Miami Lake in the evenings.

"It's doing me no good at all," John said.

"Me too." I reluctantly lifted the transit and tripod and slung them over my shoulder. At home in the city she wouldn't undress in front of a window, but out in the desert she'd stand naked thigh-deep in Miami Lake in front of us and half a dozen Dinosaur Men. Invisibility, as any lizard will tell you, is a relative thing.

I stood up on that narrow ledge, shielding the binoculars from the new light breaking over Gonzalitos, and stretched, then sat on the ledge and let my legs dangle. The sun had caught me and the rock was warming. Soon it would grow uncomfortable. I lifted the binoculars and swept them across the empty basin and then brought the focus back, reluctantly, to Caliope's town.

John was busy again, measuring and sawing boards. He had his shirt off and his head lowered over a sawhorse and his work. I watched his brown shoulders, one rock-still and one driving the saw's downstroke, and with an effort I mustered up the rip of new wood and smell of sawdust as it blew up in a small cloud around his face. Fancy. But I sneezed and brushed at my eyes.

Caliope was striped in a tangle of sunwhite boards and their shadows. The parts of her in the light glittered. I thought for a moment that she, too, had shucked her shirt and stood as half-naked as John, but it was only a trick of the light. I moved through the bars of sunlight and shade until I found the Hitch, a convert to Caliope's strange vision. She hadn't Caliope's grace, or her determination either, and was sitting with her legs stretched out in a shaded corner, guarding her eyes with one hand and looking directly into my binoculars. Perhaps a glint from the lenses or one of my small movements against the rock's face had given me away. I shifted back to Caliope, and then to John, and both of them had now stopped and were facing me. I ignored them and turned the glasses back to the Hitch.

She'd only been here a week. A huge magnet in the earth was drawing strangers to our desert. They come like this, sometimes, in a swarm like the meteor showers in August, and usually pass again as quickly and leave little sign of their having come. The Hitch was the most recent of these little human rocks to fall into this place.

She had slung her sleeping bag almost on the porch steps (she must have seen our light the night before, from below, and been drawn to it) and was curled up in it, an orange lump. I had hoped—fleetingly, ungenerously—that a scorpion or diamondback had crawled in with him (I thought her a him at first, one of these longhaired spiritual-seeking frauds who wander America's empty places), but as I watched the lump moved, rolled over, and exposed a tangle of long, dirty yellow hair.

"You're trespassing," I said. "Roll on out of there, and roll on out of here." If I didn't watch it, I'd get to be like Wilkens, the rancher who shot at pickups with out-of-state license plates. "Come on out."

I heard a muffled answer—mostly yawn—and a head popped out of the bag; not the long-nosed, weak-eyed, bearded head I'd expected, but the thin face of a very pretty girl.

I sipped my morning coffee and tried to get back the glare that I'd lost. It's hard for me to be as belligerent as I'd like.

"Is that coffee?"

I am unable to scare people. I am unable, even, to make them contrite. I gave in. "Want a cup?"

"Yes, please."

It was going to be a hot, cloudy, windy day, a sweaty, sand-blown one, the kind that John and I never work in anymore. When I brought her a cup she was still wrapped in her sleeping bag but sitting up, now, on the porch. Her hair blew across her face as she turned to take the coffee. I thought she must be roasting in that orange bag.

"Thanks."

I sat down next to her. "Traveling alone?"

"Sure."

"From where to where?"

"From here to there," she said and smiled at me, pleased with her wit.

"And from there to here, I suppose."

"Sure."

"How long have you been at it?"

"Ten days. A week."

The bag and the heavy blue Kelty pack at her feet were new and expensive. Not a poet, I decided. Not a flower child. A bored rich kid, probably, on her own for the summer before school starts. But summer was gone—or going quickly—and schools were beginning everywhere.

When she finished the coffee she put the cup down carefully next to her bag, showing a long, sun-red naked arm. She tucked it in again smoothly and sat, an orange lump again, not talking.

"What's your name?"

"Lucky," she said.

When had I ever been as young as that, hanging onto a silly name, curled up in a sleeping bag on some stranger's porch, unafraid of the world or anybody in it? When I was twelve. "How long do you plan to stay in Horse Thief Gap?"

"Is that a town near here?"

"That is here."

"Maybe a day or two," she said, watching for my reaction, playing games with the old man in the funny-looking house.

"You've got food and water?"

She shook her head.

"Warm clothes?"

She shook it again.

"Good thick boots?"

"No."

"Then a day or two," I said, getting up, "ought to be plenty."

"You won't take me in?" She opened her gray eyes as wide as they would go and tried to look innocent, or forlorn, or maybe sexy. I'd forgotten the things young girls try to do with their eyes. She had no makeup, no curl in her hair, no jewelry that I could see, but her face was far from plain; she gave me a tiny, pouty smile of the kind that stares out of cheap, four-color photographs, the kind of smile that probably worked wonders on her daddy.

"Is that an offer?"

"Not really," she said. The little girl disappeared. "No."

"There's someone here that might," I said. "Take you in, that is."

"Your son?"

I wanted to kick her and then pick her up—bag and all—and throw her twenty feet. I wanted to turn my back and walk into the house and bolt the door against her and all the people and places that make girls like that.

"There's a young woman doing her college work," I said, "over that way a mile or two." I pointed. "Her name's Caliope. She'll probably want some work out of you, though, if she feeds you."

I went on inside then and banged things around in the kitchen like an angry housewife will and realized—not for the first time; re-realized—that I was rusty around people and overreacting. I felt foolish. Even with John anymore I say or do, or don't say or don't do, the wrong things. This damned hermitage might be the wrong way to spend a life.

When I came back out to retrieve the cup she was gone. I spotted the blue pack in the wormy heat, bobbing and weaving in the haze, and I looked at it until I had to close my eyes. It stayed a spot of color on the dark insides of my eyelids.

I put the glasses down and rubbed a hand across my face. I haven't given Caliope enough credit for what she's doing. At least she knows her town is a sham, that it has no substance, but I haven't been able to admit to myself that my life is too similar to storefronts in a gully waiting for a flood. I stood, my knees popping, and climbed the rest of the way up Rayado.

I counted four vehicles I didn't know from the top of the mesa, one of which might be a white Jeep Wagoneer that belonged to the Dinosaur Men. That left three unidentified desert objects, just passing through, I hoped, having pulled off old 25 for a picnic with the kids, or a scenic stop, or to stretch the legs and look for arrowheads and agates, or to travel the back roads to Pueblo that aren't on the maps.

John and I had found a woman once, up to her hub-caps in snow, who rolled down her window and stared at us with the glazed eyes of the solidly drunk and asked us as clearly as you please if we could direct her to the turn-pike to Los Angeles. She was most of two states away. She said her daughter was having a baby—tonight—and she had to be with her. I'd gotten in behind the wheel, push-ing her gently over to the passenger's side, and I drove her into Trinidad and checked her into a motel for the night. She was asleep before I got the door unlocked. John has a theory that this place pulls, like gravity, the people who need to be here. I think this desert is a waiting room, a lobby for the lost, but neither theory makes us any more tolerant of strangers, and I wished he were standing with me instead of mingling with the guests.

I flicked the glasses in all directions, feeling nineteen again on top of a numbered hill in Korea, full of a misun-derstood responsibility and looking for any movement that I could pass on to the sergeant, who wasn't much older than I, or better yet, finish my watch and go back to the hole I'd dug and sink into it noisily so I wouldn't get shot by the high-strung, sleepless boy I shared it with.

Some men are born to being grunts as others are to riches, or polio, and there's little choice. When I thought I'd been relieved from it forever and was told to drive an ambulance for a week or so before getting on the ship to go home, I'd picked up a soldier who was holding, like a child with a doll in her arms, his own blown-off foot. That had been John, of course, and our futures were married by the Chinese mortar round that landed on him, and my GMC ambulance, and a turn in the road and one of our own mines, sunk there for all I know by a boy from Chicago who later died, or didn't, or was promoted, or went home and got married and raised children without once thinking of all the damage that two-pound lump of scrap iron had done. I wonder sometimes late at night how many of the mines we've planted are still waiting to explode.

The girls and the bombs reminded me of still another incident that's been buried for years. A man named William Hostler bred quarterhorses, the same as Wilkens does now. He's long dead by this time, but in our early years here he'd been one of our few neighbors, and he'd come by once a month or so, on a Saturday night, trailing his retarded son on an invisible leash. When Hostler sat, his son sat; when Hostler stood, his son stood; when Hostler walked to the edge of the cliff next to the out-house to piss, his son walked there, too, and stood next to his father with his penis in his hand, and he'd look around and back at us with a vacant, happy look. His name was Rob. He was twenty-three when we first got to the desert.

Hostler had only Rob and a dozen horses. He was re-tired, he said, from a life of sales, but what kind of sales he never said. He didn't look much like any salesman I ever met, but perhaps he'd used up all his smiles years ago, or had given them, as a legacy, to his idiot son. He was tall and thin with huge hands and ears and wore a crewcut, as we did. The tooth next to his canine was as black as obsidian, and his nose was cratered. I thought of syphilis every time I saw him.

The boy, besides being retarded, was wall-eyed and fat and moved with that peculiar gait you sometimes see in such people, a shuffle that brought his foot forward without lifting it. He'd plant it firmly before dragging the next one alongside, and you knew that each sliding step required a conscious design. He would look around smugly—and perhaps rightfully so—when he'd gotten to where he'd started out for.

Once a month Hostler would take his son into Trinidad, in Colorado. He bought groceries and whatever else he needed, bought his son a beer, and got them both laid.

"Go into Snakepit with us tonight?" he said once when he stopped by our place for a free beer. Rob sat in the righthand seat of their old one-ton flatbed, grinning like his father, with his left hand in the air cradling an imaginary steering wheel.

Snakepit was the name of a bar tacked onto the front of a whorehouse where the locals bet on the fights between rattlesnakes and kings on Saturday nights.

"For the boy, too?" I asked.

"Sure for the boy, too. He's grown, isn't he?"

I hadn't been to a cathouse since Tokyo. I hadn't smelled a woman for a year. There'd been a couple of girls in college (for me, anyway; I don't know about John), but nobody since, and the heat and the loneliness of the desert were starting to bring unwanted daylight dreams.

I asked John what he thought, and he surprised me. "Sure," he said.

"We could all go in your Jeep," Hostler said. He had terrible tires on his truck, and whenever he made the trip into town he and the boy were threatened with walking. He patched the blowouts with bootsoles and glue.

So we took the old Jeep we had in those days, and when we pulled up in front of Snakepit John started laughing. He fiddled with his crutches to give the Hostlers time to get in front of us. "You know," he said, when they were out of earshot, "this is a hell of a thing."

"Nervous?"

He shook his head. "I was thinking about the whores. Can you imagine them looking out the upstairs window and seeing the four of us pile out?"

"What about it?"

"A drooling, retarded fat kid about to wet his pants," he said, holding up a finger. "A horny old bastard with a black tooth and breath like horses. You, sort of normal, but who knows? And me, stumping along on one leg." He looked at the four fingers he had raised and shook his head. "A whore's life in Trinidad can't be an easy one."

"What whore's life is?"

"There's call girls in New York City or Boston that would run you a hundred bucks a throw," he said. "And turn any one of us down for twice that. They've got nice manners and sweet breath."

"How do you know?"

"I had a hundred bucks to spend, once, before the war." John curled his fingers into a fist, and we went in.

"What are you having?" Hostler asked us. His son was nowhere in sight.

"Beer," John said for both of us.

"The boy's upstairs."

It struck me then that if the boy had a mother his life might be bleaker. He'd never been as far as Albuquerque and had no thoughts larger than feeding horses. Lucky for him his father had the good sense to buy him something he'd seen the stock do.

But it should have been different for John and me.

A large, black-haired Indian woman came down the stairs and picked up Hostler's whiskey glass with a thumb and forefinger, then went back up. Hostler gave us a wink and followed her. That left an old man sitting alone at one table talking to himself, the bartender—a kid of twelve— and the two of us.

"Big-city night life," John said.

"There's snake fights later."

"Oh boy."

"I wonder how Rob's getting along."

"Rob's probably getting along just fine. They must know him here."

"How about us?" I asked. "How are we getting along?" We had a year behind us in this awful place.

John, for some reason I've never been able to figure out, stuck a finger in his beer like a blind man checking its level. "We don't have to stay here," he said. "If you want to go, let's go."

"I don't mean here. I mean New Mexico."

"I know what you mean."

"What about the maps for Arlyle?"

"Screw 'em," he said, licking his finger. "Or finish them first, and quit. Or survey ground for new ones. *Or do them all wrong.*" He turned towards me on his barstool. "It doesn't matter to me."

"That's what worries me, John. It doesn't matter to me either."

"Then leave it," he said. "We'll go when we want. We've got dollars piling up in the bank in Raton and a job with its own hours."

We drank our beers and ordered two more. The big Indian woman came down again and appraised us. She took a seat next to the old man, who never noticed her.

"You going upstairs?" John asked.

"It's why we came. Aren't you?"

"I wouldn't mind."

"Then go ahead."

He signaled the woman, as a man will a waitress, and she took him up. I thought I'd go, too, but I decided to wait for Rob so he wouldn't be sitting alone.

Hostler came down, but his son didn't. "Whiskey," he said, and took his old seat. "Is the boy still upstairs?"

"I guess."

He nodded.

"Maybe I'll go look for him," I said.

"He's all right."

"Maybe I'll go up anyway."

He winked at me and hunched over his drink and said something in Spanish to the boy behind the bar.

I went up. The old Indian woman was sitting on an ancient sofa on the landing, listening to a radio and knitting. She put a pile of blue yarn down and gave me a big crooked smile. The side of her face farthest from me looked caved in, as if the teeth and jaw were missing underneath.

"You want to see?"

I shook my head. That was the worst of it, I remembered. In Korea they'd lined up all the small-breasted, skinny girls only half dressed and we'd stood there and pointed at the ones we wanted, like choosing pastries or puppies. I wanted to avoid that; I don't remember any of the Korean girls, but I remember having to choose them.

I paid her with a five, and ones. A roll of quarters would have done it.

She whistled. A girl put her head out a doorway. "Carmen," she said, and pointed.

Carmen was a short, fairly slim, dark-haired woman of about twenty-five. (Now, looking back, I can see a resemblance to Caliope, unless I have given Caliope's features to the girl in my memory.) She was dressed in boy's jeans and a checked flannel shirt. I had thought the girls would be sitting around in negligees. She looked me up and down as if the choosing went both ways, then reached out and gripped my belt, gave it a tug, let go of it again, and walked down the hall.

When I got downstairs again, John and Hostler were talking about horses.

"Where's Rob?"

"He'll be down in a minute," his father said.

And sure enough, a minute later he ran downstairs and tucked his face shyly into his father's shoulder. The corners of his mouth were wet and his nose was running. We had one more drink, decided not to stay for the snake fights, and piled into the Jeep to go home.

"Did you have fun, boy?" Hostler asked his son.

Rob nodded and kept nodding, all the way back, his neck on a spring like a jack-in-the-box.

"I guess he did," John said. "He was at it long enough."

"Rob just watches," Hostler said. He slapped his son on the back and laughed. "They let him look into the rooms for ten dollars."

After a minute of quiet driving, John said, "Don't come by our place again."

One of us should have hit Hostler. John didn't because he was at the wheel, or because he would have killed him. I didn't because I didn't want to lose my fist in that crater.

Neither of us has gone back. The old Indian woman is dead by now or has become one of those photographic negatives the desert produces—white hair surrounding a stone-black face—and the boy bartender has grown into a fat, middle-aged man of forty and the girl is long gone to whatever future Trinidad whores have. Maybe they've replaced the sand and the snakes in the pit with Jell-O or motor oil and they bet on the women. I don't want to know. Civilization is something we haven't gotten yet.

I walked back across the mesa top, hunched down against the blowing grit, to one of our benchmarks. We'd set this one in our first year, 1957, the year they put Sputnik up. Seven thousand four hundred and five feet. I wondered if this hill was hollowed out, as the mountains were, as my life seemed to be, and we just hadn't found the entrance to it yet. If Gonzalitos were hollow, I could crawl down into its bowels and wait for the Dinosaur Men to peel away its face with their picks and find my face staring out.

Me, crammed in with the dinosaurs. But what then? Boo?

3

"Hot work," John said at lunch when he came back in to wash up, and I guessed he meant the sawing and hammering and not the ten minutes he'd just spent sitting in the outhouse. He brought a sandwich and a glass of lemonade out of the kitchen.

"Why are you doing it?"

"I told you, for the lumber."

Right. "I counted four buildings up this morning," I said. "How many are there in a town?"

"Depends on the town. Hotel, jail, bar, grocery store, gas station." He ticked them off on his fingers. "Five."

"Hotel with bar," I said. "No jail. Grocery store in the gas station. Two?"

"It's women building it," he said. "Two jails, no bar, three hotels, two groceries, and half a dozen clothing stores. What's that? Thirteen?"

I sat back. "Churches. She'll have to build at least one."

"And a city hall."

"Any real town would have a whorehouse."

"That's in one of the hotels," John said. "I know the desk clerk." He gave me a funny look, maybe remembering, as I had, Snakepit. "Why don't you come down after lunch and see?"

Had he put any weight on *come down?* I decided he hadn't. "I've never cared a lot for towns," I said. "Even imaginary ones. Besides, it's her place." And maybe yours.

It was being parceled out: a chunk for them, a slice for the Dinosaur Men, our house and the caves for us, and all the rest of it in dispute, trespassed on by all sides. Perhaps when all the bones had been pulled up and packed into crates and the rains had come and washed the town away and the prospectors had dug out everything valuable it would be left to us again. But at the moment they all had claims as good as ours, and they were working theirs.

Even with our surveying finished, as it appeared to be for now, we are held here by some terrible responsibility. It's a custodial one, maybe, having received the loan for this part of the world, or maybe we're prisoners to the color and geometry of the land.

But the geometry was off in lots of ways. When we'd spied on Caliope we'd been reshooting ground we'd shot years before, and, oddly, we were coming up with new numbers. John checked them against our earlier notes that night and found discrepancies.

"Four feet at benchmark one-eleven," he said. "Four feet!"

"Up or down?"

He gave me a look that said, What difference does that make? but said, "Up."

"When did we shoot it?"

"October tenth and eleventh, 1978."

"Maybe we were drunk."

"For two days?"

"In 1978."

"I think the ground's moving on us," he said.

"Sloppy surveying."

"No."

"Earthquakes, then," I said. "They happen."

"No."

"All those subterranean pressures." I scratched my thigh, pulled at my groin, and stuck my tongue out.

He stared at me. "No."

"What, then?"

"Let's reshoot it in the morning."

We did, and we were still four feet away from the good numbers. We shot again the creekbeds and the level places and the basaltic outcrops that couldn't have shifted without shaking apart.

"So we made an error," I said, "somewhere in the '70s."

He shook his head but hadn't a better answer.

I should have gone down with him after lunch to look at the new town, but I decided instead to visit the Dinosaur Men.

The Dinosaur Men had crept in quietly one night and

set up their tents without us knowing. They were in the desert two days before we discovered them following us, and they pulled up from the ground toe bones and horns and whatnot, counting on—somehow knowing—that the earth changed wherever we set the tripod down and trained the glass.

John and I once thought we'd fooled them. We took our tools out onto a piece of tableland we knew by heart and set about our chore. There was nothing under our feet but rock. A Dinosaur Man sniffed around and called the others in, and soon the whole tribe was sitting in a circle about a half mile off, waiting. We took our time, which isn't easy when you've nothing to do, and finally packed it in at dusk. In the morning we went back out, but they were already roping and staking and digging shallow, one-foot holes in a gridded square, excited as kids. One of them—McIntyre—walked over to us and leaned on his shovel, grinning. It turned out they'd found about a thousand turtle shells, all that remained of a whole migration that had died for some reason on an old sea bottom. After that, John and I had to accept that we are prophets, or lodestones—some sort of strange compasses, anyway—to the Dinosaur Men.

But trouble came when we stupidly headed for our monkey puzzle—a triangulation point on Kit Carson Mesa—and the land turned over as it was doing lately and exposed a skeletal hand. We didn't see it, but the Dinosaur Men jumped on it, crouching on all fours as predators will.

I could see the finger bones in the rock: a hand stratum. How many times had John and I sat under that monkey puzzle? A thousand times—two thousand times— and I swear that hand hadn't been there. We couldn't help but feel that a magic was at work: the land rising up on four feet to call attention to itself and then rolling over and giving up its dead.

"It isn't that," the Dinosaur Man said. "It's a matter of seeing."

I told him I hadn't seen a fossil in my whole life.

"You have to know what to look for," he said. "It takes a trained eye."

My eye's as trained as any, and I told him so. He said he'd show me it wasn't, and about a week later he came up to where I was sitting. He had an old .22 rifle in his hand, scarred at the stock and rusty at the sight. He handed it to me with a box of shells.

"Put half the box in the air," he said. "All in the same direction."

I chose north and did as he asked. He took the rifle from me and fired the other twenty-five rounds in the same place, trying to match my elevation.

"Let's go find the bullets," he said.

I've got a good eye for distance, so I walked to where I judged I should and started looking. I stared at the ground for an hour and felt foolish.

"I've got the wrong spot, I guess," I said.

He'd been right behind me the whole time. He

opened his palm and spilled half a dozen of the dull lead pellets into my hand.

As long as I live, I won't forget this, I thought, and it must have shown on my face because he laughed at my look. "You go to the right spot," he said. "You just don't see anything once you get there."

That was after they dug up the hand, and the arm that came with it, and they had no choice, they said, but to burrow under the tree for the rest of it.

"Not under our tree," John said.

"We have to get all of it."

"Not from under that monkey puzzle."

They called a committee meeting and stood off in a huddle for fifteen minutes. "Peters thinks we can get what we need without uprooting it," McIntyre said.

John said no.

"We could watch them," I told him.

"And do what? Catch it when it falls over?" But after a great deal of glaring and grumbling and biceps-flexing, he gave in.

They went at it carefully and pulled legs out after two days' work, and a handful of bones that were the feet, and then the pelvis was unearthed, looking for all the world like an old horse collar, and they collected a bagful of walnuts that was the spine, and then the other arm. It was while they were digging for the skull that McIntyre brought his rifle around and showed me the trick with the bullets.

Their excavation went slowly. They built a small tunnel, shoring it with fruit-crate slats, leaving the long, gnarled roots of the monkey puzzle embedded in their own soil. I got down in it, at their invitation, and squirmed inside. It was only two feet high, and my shoulders brushed the shoring. I took a light and went in on my back. The wooden veins in the rocky soil formed an arch in the low ceiling, and though the tunnel was only a day or two old it felt older, spookier. Getting out required hollering and being tugged out by my ankles.

"We'll pack the tunnel again before closing it up," McIntyre said.

"Are you giving up, then?"

"Not on your life. There's a skull in there we want."

"Maybe the corpse was decapitated," John said, "and you're wrecking the place for nothing."

"We're being careful; look for yourself."

The tunnel wasn't wide enough for him, but I doubt if he would have gone down in it anyway.

"It's not likely the head's missing," McIntyre said. "That's a European custom. And an Asian one."

"The Spanish were here for centuries. They still are," John said. "Long enough to teach the Indians something of that."

McIntyre gave John a long look, and I swear I could see the decision being made in his head. "Primitive men didn't cut each other's heads off," he said. "They bashed them in."

"How old is this guy?"

"Girl. We have her pelvis. We'll run tests when we get back, but if we had the skull, I—Peters—could tell you right now."

"What makes you think she isn't just another old Indian?"

"Are either of you geologists?"

We shook our heads. We can tell limestone from sandstone and granite from lava, but that's not what he meant and we knew it.

"This is old rock," he said, lifting a handful of the tunnel spoil. "I'd guess what's in there might be ten thousand years old."

"That's too old for Indians?" I asked.

John, to my surprise, nodded.

"Are you changing sides?" I asked him.

He shook his head. "I took art history classes," he said. "Ten thousand years ago we were just leaving off drawing pictures on cave walls."

"And domesticating the dog," McIntyre added.

They spent two weeks in that tunnel without unearthing a skull. They closed it up, regretfully, replacing the loose soil and tamping it down as they'd promised with a wooden club. I tried to keep my pleasure from showing when I told them, honestly, that I was sorry they hadn't gotten what they'd wanted.

"It's here somewhere," McIntyre said. "Peters'll get it. It's not under the tree roots, is all."

"Where is it, then?"

He shrugged. "The right hand was flung up, so." He demonstrated. "The skull could have been close enough— here—to have eroded out." He looked down the slope to the dry creekbed that ran along the bottom. "We'll search every inch of that," he said, and neither of us doubted him.

Two of them began it the next afternoon, walking the white flint riverbed in a leisurely, hunched-over way, hoping to catch the domed curve of skull pretending to be a stone, or the plierslike pincer of jaw of that long-dead girl. They walked the four miles to Miami Lake, where the creekbed emptied, and found Caliope swimming.

The two young men brought her back to the site under the monkey puzzle, and introductions were made. John and I nodded another hello. The young Dinosaur Men were anxious to tell the tale of finding her but couldn't with her beside them. They grinned at each other behind her back. She'd been naked, of course. Caliope wanted to go to their camp and see the girl bones, and we agreed, after a little urging, to go too and hear Peters lecture.

Their camp was eight green canvas tents set up in a rough rectangle on the east side of Stagecoach Hill. Somebody knew his business: they had shade in the afternoons, and it would stay dry even in heavy rain. Peters and McIntyre had tents to themselves, the four young men in their party doubled, and then on the perimeter they'd set up a mess tent, another for storage, and two large work tents they used when the weather was bad or too hot. We were ushered into one of these, fitted out with picnic tables and long benches, and John and I took seats near the flap. McIntyre lit hurricane lamps and passed around cold bottles of Pabst.

Peters sat on one of the long tables and held up a bone. "A woman's humerus," he said. "She stood four foot eight and wasn't as old as you are now, dear," he said to Caliope. Caliope allowed him a big, slow smile that would have warned me off. "She had arthritis," Peters said, glancing at Caliope still. "And she was buried with some ceremony."

"How do you know that?" Caliope asked. She slurred a stress between the *you* and the *know* just slight enough to maintain an innocent inquiry.

There was something catty going on between the two of them and Peters seemed to enjoy it. "Which that do you mean, dear?" he asked, purring. I looked into that fat, smug face and shivered. McIntyre, somewhat younger than Peters, still has that intense collegiate excitement that the younger ones have (that we had once, I thought) and the wiry build the desert gives you, but Peters—even though he was obviously comfortable in the field, out in the open—looked as if he hadn't been in the light for long. It wasn't only that he was old and slow and pale; he had an indefiniteness in his eyes, as if he believed in nothing. Something about the way he held his hands struck me as matronly. This innuendo with Caliope wasn't lechery—or even honest lust—but seemed feminine: in him, twisted, wrong. He seemed to be coaxing Caliope into a fight, or a trap. If spiders could talk, I thought.

"That she was buried with some ceremony," Caliope said to his question.

"Because of this."

A blue pebble was passed from hand to hand until it reached Caliope. I leaned forward and looked over her shoulder. I pretended to look at the stone, but I was more aware of her neck and the smell of her and of the shadow the lamp threw on a curve of breast that I wanted to put my hand on. She held the rock up so I could see it better, and I leaned back.

"Turquoise?" I asked.

Peters nodded. "Carved."

It looked weathered. The vague, blurry outline of a pattern on it seemed random, as if wind or water had made it.

"We found two bone needles near her hand. It's not hard to imagine her gripping them."

"Are you trying to make a case for Neanderthal?" Caliope asked.

"Certainly not. Not here in New Mexico. Wrong pelvis, for one thing."

"California Man?"

"What's that?" I asked. "Someone with lungs like large balloons?"

"California Man—" Caliope began, but Peters cut her off.

"California Man," Peters said, "is the popular name given to a find made a couple of years ago in the San Bernardino Mountains. More properly, it's called Yuha Man and was given an initial dating of seventy thousand years. That *would* be Neanderthal, certainly. But that's disputed—the date, I mean—not believed, really, by most. The dating method is, to put it gently, questionable, something called aspartic acid racemization. Not at all reliable. While there is some evidence in South America of early man thirteen thousand years old, and some in the Yukon as old as forty thousand, by all accounts early man seems to have crossed over the land bridge in Alaska about twenty-seven thousand years ago."

One of the young men coughed politely.

"And even that is disputable," Peters said, smiling. He tilted his head and the lantern light caught his glasses, giving a strange, flattened shape to his head. He looked lemurlike, with large, yellow, glowing eyes. "That's too far back, I think. Ten thousand years is quite enough to make this find"—he waved the humerus like a drumstick—"exciting. If we're lucky, this is Clovis."

"New Mexico Man," John said. "Sangre de Cristo Man."

I knew what John was thinking: there is an Indian burial place at Tooth of Time Ridge in the Sangre de Cristos. I'd never seen it; it was a place he went to alone, but he talked about it often in oblique references, and he'd promised to take me there someday.

"That has a nice sound to it," Peters said.

"But you're not sure she's that old?"

"We can't be sure of anything until we date her. And the skull would help us a great deal." He looked at John as if he suspected he'd hidden the thing.

Date her, I thought.

"You don't have it yet?" Caliope asked. What had the young Dinosaur Men talked to her about on the long walk back from Miami Lake? Well, I guess I wouldn't have talked to a woman stranger I'd just seen naked about the skull of a dead one, either.

"No. Not yet."

It was a threat, pointed right at us. John and I have the same hideous vision of yellow bulldozers and backhoes, a swarm of pickups, and a small town springing up crowded with archaeologists. Let's hope, I thought, that she's a murdered Indian whose skull was carried off as a prize by conquistadores or a rival tribe.

Peters talked on and said something about bringing a team in and bringing the tree down (I missed a lot of that; I was watching Caliope's shoulder blades move under her singlet as she sipped her beer and wishing I were sitting where Peters was), and John said something to him I didn't catch and stood up to go. He caught me with his eyes. I saw those bulldozers in them. I got up to go with him.

"What's so important about keeping the tree?" Caliope asked him, but he ignored her and went out. She looked at me.

"Come by after breakfast, and I'll show it to you," I said.

"I've seen it."

"Maybe."

"When's breakfast?"

"Let's say eight."

"I should be working by then."

I shrugged. I shouldn't bother. I didn't care if she was on our side or not; I wanted only to watch her climb the mesa and help her, maybe, when she slipped. My head was filling so fast with fantasies I couldn't sort them, and I left, catching up with John at the truck.

"They'll take the tree down," he said when I got in.

"Maybe not."

"You're letting the enemy into our camp."

"She's not the enemy yet."

"She will be, Paul. You can't compete with men half your age." He was quiet, then, all the way back. "Don't bring her into the house," he said when we got home. "Do what you want, but not that."

"Okay, John."

I did bring her into the house, and that knocked everything crooked, but before I'd done that John had driven across the dawn-dark desert at four in the morning and stolen every last bone from the Dinosaur Men, including the bag of fingers.

A red-faced McIntyre, two students-turned-henchmen, and the large, loose, slow-moving Peters had beaten on the door at six-thirty the next morning. I would have asked them in except for John hobbling up behind me and banging a crutch against my leg. It may have looked accidental to the Dinosaur Men, but John puts those crutches where he wants.

So I said, "Good morning," and waited.

It was plain that McIntyre wanted to speak, but Peters, nearer our age and patience, put a hand on his shoulder. "Good morning," Peters said. I remembered, looking at him, that he, like us, had spent his life in places like this, sifting sand and stone for small important things and tapping rocks apart with his tiny hammer. Clearly he expected to be asked in, after his hospitality to us the night before, and John, recognizing this, edged past me onto the porch and sat on the rail. He, too, was good at knocking things apart with small strokes.

It's a good house we have now, that we've added to over the years, expanded from the one adobe room we'd built to weather our first New Mexico winter. We have four rooms: a kitchen with a good wood cookstove, a living room, and two bedrooms, and outside we've built a long, wide, covered porch—a veranda—in the Spanish style and a shed, for the real work.

"Coffee?" I asked, holding up my cup.

"No, thanks." This was business. "The bones are gone," Peters said without any more politeness. "All of them. We wondered if you'd know why"—I started to interrupt him, but he rode the rest of his sentence over the top of my objection—"being that you've been here so long. There might be thieves about that you'd know of," he said softly, and I caught that same undercurrent of two messages that I'd heard the night before when he was speaking to Caliope.

This time, I knew what they both meant. I'd heard John go out early.

"Maybe coyotes," I said.

John nodded, propping up the bad lie. "Dogs and bones," he said.

"These are more rock than bone," Peters said.

I shrugged. "Packrats, then. When we first got here, packrats stole us blind. Two years after I lost it, we found my wristwatch in one of their nests. The band had been severed as cleanly as a jeweler could do it and was woven into the nest's floor matting."

"Are they big rats?"

I spread my hands apart. A foot.

"Her pelvis has the heft of a bowling ball," Peters said. "It's packed with sediments like cement."

I moved out onto the porch, then, and let the screen door close behind me. "I didn't take them, if that's what you're asking. Theft out here is a serious complaint."

McIntyre took a step forward, but Peters stopped him this time by speaking. "We're just asking for your help," he said. "You know the people around here; we don't. That girl's remains are as important to us—to me, actually—as that monkey puzzle is to you. I'm sure you understand that."

"We do," I said. "But we don't know any bone thieves."

Peters smiled, nodded at John, who hadn't moved from the porch rail, nodded at me, still smiling, and turned McIntyre with a large hand as a father might a boy. The two men climbed down the steps and the other two followed them to their Jeep. But it seemed to me that the four left ghosts behind standing in their footprints.

"Where are they?" I asked John out of the corner of my mouth.

He waited until their Jeep started. "In my room," he said. "I was going to throw them in the lake, but then I thought the caves would be better."

"You could warn me next time," I said, waving goodbye to the Dinosaur Men.

"You did fine," he said.

"What if I'd let them in?"

"Into my room?"

"No, of course not."

"Well, then?"

"Yeah. Well, then." I finished my coffee and tipped the cup upside down to let the last cold bit of it drop into the dust. "Want to go now?"

"You invited the girl over after breakfast," John said.

"She won't come."

"All right," he said, after a minute. "The sooner the better, don't you think?"

"Yes."

John brought the bones out in a canvas bag and dropped them into the pickup bed. Peters was right; they sounded like rocks, but then I wasn't sure I knew what a bag of bones sounded like. John got in behind the wheel. The truck had an automatic transmission, but John had driven even in the old days by shifting without the clutch. He had the ear that long-haul truckers develop and could change gears on the engine's revs as smoothly as I could with the pedal. But it still could get tricky on hills, and in town with all the stoplights and such.

"I hope Caliope doesn't show up now," he said, and put the truck in gear.

I looked at him, and the bones in the back. "I hope the sheriff doesn't."

4

We'd misjudged the strength and speed of the brewing clouds and had found the caves by running from the hailstorm. The coffee-colored sky sent down a scatter of knuckly hail without thunder, and John and I were caught flatfooted. The truck was miles away, but the mountain was at hand, so we worked ourselves into a fold of it, caught in a crossfire as the hail ricocheted off the rock. We protected our eyes the best we could and inched backward against the rock like crabs, and I remember thinking that the transit was doomed.

I followed John. He took a turn, and another, and then whistled, and I saw there was an immense darkness behind us. He stepped into it, and I stepped in behind him, shaking hail from my hair.

I bought books on caverns and spelunking the next day, and they're still about somewhere, probably under John's bed, where most of our library ends up. I've forgotten the geology that makes caves, except that it's limestone and water, but the picture I've retained from that long-ago reading is one of bats a foot thick on the ceilings and a knee-deep, hip-deep mud of bat guano shifting like quicksand as the beetles crawl through it, the waste of the one the food for the other, and in the pools under the stalactites are blind, white animals that must fish among themselves for their suppers.

Our caves have no bats. The ceilings are high, vaulted, cathedral-like, flecked and shimmering with mica. They are humped hollows under the Sangre de Cristo Mountains, running east and west across the range. The bright, hot New Mexico colors here are darkened, but still present as mysterious pastel shades, oddly tinted in the light of lanterns.

I had an aunt we'd visit on holidays when I was growing up. She painted landscapes in a high attic room, and she let me watch sometimes if I was quiet and stayed out of her light. She sat in a high-backed kitchen chair, pushing the canvas away from her with a stiff brush, and when she was done with the painting she'd pass her hand over it, still with the brush at the ends of her fingers, and darken it somehow as only artists can. These caves reminded me of Aunt Margaret's paintings. If the Indians had known this place, they'd left nothing of theirs behind, or else they'd darkened it enough that we hadn't found it yet.

An underground river runs through here year-round, though now, in September, it was low and the brine from higher watermarks was plain on the walls where it had

pooled, in flood, and rushed southeast into and under
Texas, perhaps all the way to the Gulf. The caves
stretched for miles, and we'd always meant to buy a raft
and visit all the rooms, but we never had. Water, underground and in the dark, holds a menace that isn't easily
dispelled; if we got the light, and the raft, and the time,
we'd do it one day.

We stood just inside the entrance, a doorway into the
hill that you enter standing, a fissure in the rock like the
sand fly on a desert tent: a passage of baffles that in two
quick turnings cuts off the light and the outside. How
much of the earth is hollow?

John, in these circumstances, was forced to follow me.
I held the lantern out to light the way for him, and he
limped behind, banging the sack of bones against his
crutches.

"What do you have in mind?" I asked. Even whisper-
ing, our voices rolled in here, bouncing off the high, dark
ceiling and returning to us as grumbles and noise.

"The sulphur pool."

"Hiding them isn't enough?"

"No."

The sulphur pool is one of several hotsprings, but un-
like the others it is an evil-smelling fumarole ringed with
white and yellow crystals. Its water is thick and dark, hiding its bottom from the strongest light we could shine into
it. John dropped the bones in, bag and all.

"That's that," he said.

I grinned at him and probably looked demonic. "There's still the skull."

"When they find that," he said, "we'll steal it and drop it in, too."

"You've forced their hand, John. They'll have to bring the tree down now, hunting for it."

"They would have anyway. And even that's better than the circus they would have brought here when they got the test back on those bones."

"You're betting they're old enough to cause a fuss?"

"Yes."

We both stared after them, into that dark soup. If that she-skeleton was a hundred centuries old, she was irreplaceable, and we'd done a terrible thing. It was a sad, undignified end. Still, I reminded myself, if she was a hundred years old, or a hundred months, it was still a sad, undignified end. Anybody's bones deserve better than we gave them.

Then again, perhaps we'd brought her home.

"Swim?" John asked.

"Bath, for me."

Four pools were heated by the same hotspring that made the sulphur cauldron, and we use them for baths when we visit. I splashed into the clear water of one of them while John eased into the river. I sank down to my chin. The water pulled the knots of years from my shoulders and relieved, a bit, the ache Caliope had given me.

John yelled as always when he hit the river, and in the dark I could see John's stump in my mind, puckered and square where they'd tied it off just below the hip, and the scars that run up his back like zippers. Not a pretty man, John, but my only friend for much of my life.

John rose dripping out of the river.

"Don't get into the wrong one."

He dropped into the pool next to me. "This desert's getting pretty damned crowded," he said after a time.

"Overpopulated," I agreed.

"There's us and them and the girl," he said.

"And the ranchers."

"And Miami, a hundred and fifty strong."

"Strangers, all of them."

"And the prospectors," he said. "There's always one or two of them around."

"And Jamieson."

"And the rockhounds that come out on weekends about now."

"And the kids with the motorized trikes."

The first time we'd seen one of those, we had been transported back to the pictures we'd seen of men on the moon in July of 1969. "Look what you've missed," John had said. "First Sputnik, and now the moon." But I'd never have chosen space to do my engineering in. It was bridges I'd wanted to build, once, and never would now; bridges, but not across those distances.

"Noisy bastards," John said.

I waited for a bit, thinking about noisy bastards. I stretched my ankles and knees and heard them creak. I rocked my shoulders back and forth in the pool, causing currents. "You're going to head out for a bit, aren't you?"

"Yes."

"With or without me?"

"Without, I think,"

"Okay." I couldn't have known then that in a week he'd decide to pack up everything important to him, get a leg and a girl, and maybe not come back.

He went on these solitary hikes more often than I. A day under the monkey puzzle would even out the world for me. He'd take the pickup, of course, and our traveling tent, and enough food for two days, and he'd stay gone for a week or more, coming back pounds lighter, sometimes, but sometimes not. He said once that he trapped scorpions and boiled them like shrimp. "Tough," he said, "but the tail comes with its own toothpick."

The shape of the scorpion is always with us: it rises up in this land, in its buttes and mesas, in the bad weather that hangs on the horizon waiting to be swept in overhead, in the lightning that strikes straight down. It's my leg John wants, not a plastic one.

"Where will you go?" And then I added, "In case I need to find you."

"Tooth of Time. You won't be able to find me."

"I could find you," I said. I left that there for a minute, and then said, "It'll look like guilt."

"Well?"

Yeah, but what do I do with mine? I held the lantern

out over the sulphur pool on our way out, half expecting to see the bones bobbing up and expecting to catch, like smoke in the nose, the escaping spirit of a long-, long-dead young woman, but the pool only fumed and stank as always and belched up nothing.

John had packed and driven off (without a wave) before Caliope came by. She had on a man's work shirt of summer flannel, checked blue and black, with the sleeves rolled up and slopping around her elbows. Father's? Husband's? Boyfriend's? Brother's? Maybe she bought it at the Salvation Army for a nickel; what difference did it make? I met her on the porch and offered her coffee.

"How can you drink that in this heat? I've just walked three miles."

"It's barely ninety," I said. "It's an autumn afternoon with a chill in the air."

"Do you have a cold beer?"

"Are you old enough?"

She gave me a look that might be pity, and I went inside and got her one.

"I stayed late and it turned into a party," she said. "They like to drink. I overslept."

I waved a hand, not wanting explanations. I didn't say that I wouldn't have been here if she'd been on time.

"What's so special about your tree? Ian says you'll fight to keep it."

"Ian?"

"Ian McIntyre."

"We'd like to keep it, if it's keepable," I said. "We won't spill blood over it."

"What's so special about it?"

"I'll take you up there. We'll have to walk; John has the truck."

She groaned and sat down on the steps. "Is it far?"

"You were there yesterday."

"From the other direction," she said. "Not from here."

"A couple miles."

"I've already missed a day's work." She stood up, and sighed, and seemed to settle into her sandals. "He won't be back soon? With the truck?"

I shook my head.

"Can we take a couple of beers with us? For strength?"

"For the hangover? Sure."

It was an easy walk. We talked mostly about her studies, but when she tried to quote films to make her points, as another might literature, I had to raise my hands in surrender every time.

"What was the last film you saw?" she asked, exasperated.

I had to think a long way back. "2001, I guess."

"That must have come out fifteen years ago."

I raised my hands again. "Sorry. We probably caught it on its second or third—or thirtieth—go-around. It takes a while to get movies in Trinidad."

"No TV?"

I wanted to say, "What's TV?" but said no.

On the rough stretches I held back and let her walk ahead, and I could guess once I saw that feminine half smile that she knew exactly why, and it's true; I wouldn't have denied it if she'd confronted me in court with my lechery. Her brown hamstrings, and the bob of her dark hair, and even the sweat between her shoulder blades was exciting. Her left hip pocket had a worn, white square where a man's wallet had been stored. It was hard to believe that these were hand-me-downs. What man had a small enough waist? Little brother?

We climbed Kit Carson and came to the tree.

"Now tell me what makes it so special," she said, and sat on its root. "After you give me one or two of those beers."

I pulled one from the pack, still cold with the water that had been ice. I opened it for her, got another for me, and then took my boots off.

"See any other trees around?" I asked and didn't wait for the shake of her head. "It's a monkey puzzle. It's from Chile, I think. Planted here, for all I know, by a lunatic."

"I'd had the impression you two planted it."

I shook my head. "I wish we had. We've never added anything to this place."

She ran a hand across its bark and pulled back sharply.

"The leaves are like that, too," I said. "That's another thing I guess we like about it. It's not a soft tree." I looked at the fill the Dinosaur Men had put in, loosely packed for all their tamping, wrong-colored, lumpy, as if the hill had a cancer. "It was our first triangulation point," I said. "Our first benchmark. It's there, behind you." Though with all the digging and messing around, I thought, it's wrong now.

She swiveled around on the root, found the round brass monument, and read it aloud.

"It was here that I first got hit by lightning," I said.

"You've been struck by lightning?"

"I'm always getting hit by lightning. It's that damned instrument I carry. John manages to lay the gradestick down and lie flat." I gave her what I hoped was a lightning-struck look, just boyish enough to interest her. "You'd think with the metal sticks he hops around on—but no, it's me that gets it."

She looked at me strangely, considering, I guess, whether or not I was telling the truth. Her dark eyes had flecks of red in the pupils. Lovely.

"Honest?"

"Cross my heart."

"How many times?"

She meant the lightning. I knew, but I pretended to think about it, moving my fingers as I counted. "Seven."

"How come you're not dead?"

I shrugged. "I guess I've got the lives of a cat."

"So it's a benchmark," she said. "And a lightning rod."

"And more. It's *place*," I said.

"And out of place."

I nodded; she understood us now.

"And it had a dead girl under it," she said.

"Yes." I looked at her frankly, at the way she sat on the tree root with her knees together, at the way the late light hit her horizontally. "Do you think I stole it? Her?"

"Yes," she said. "You or your partner, or both of you to-gether."

"Is that what they think, too?"

"That's what they said last night."

"And you've taken sides."

"There aren't any sides to take," she said. "*Did* you steal it?" She grinned. "Her?"

"No."

"Did your partner?"

"You'll have to ask John that."

"You're protecting him."

Myself, too, and all of this, I wanted to say, but a girl as smart as she—almost a doctor of something-or-other—should understand something as vital as metaphor. What are we but the sum of our relationships, the interstices of our triangulation points?

"Does it matter to you what I'm doing?" I asked.

She shook her head slowly. She stood up and stretched. Ah, damn, how was I foolish enough all those years ago to give up women?

The girl was crazy, I had to remind myself. What, if not insanity, drives a beautiful girl here to labor ten hours a day building and painting storefronts, only to hope for a flood? Religion? Art? According to John they're often the same thing. But insanity, I've argued to him, is a lack, and art a fullness. He disagrees vehemently. There's a crowd in every nutcase, he says. I don't know which I believe anymore, but I can't help admitting that there is something skewed and sideways in art, too, like in my Aunt Margaret. And I remember John dropping that rock, rebuilding his face, and dropping that rock a second time. He's stubborn, but not insane.

We made our way down Kit Carson Mesa without saying anything else, and once on the flat Caliope turned and looked back at the monkey puzzle. I watched her eyes as she dismissed it, and me. I resolved right then to die in a swamp if I could manage it and hope that with enough time my bones would turn into coal. Even the Dinosaur Men know that immortality comes in long, hard shapes.

We walked the last half mile in the sharp of sunset, with our shadows thrown sideways in long, dark ribbons. As I stepped onto the front porch the sky turned black and the stars stood out clearly. Caliope would never find her way on such a night, and she hesitated now, not joining me on the porch, not turning for home.

"Beer?" I asked. "Or coffee?"

"Either one would be fine."

"Come inside." I thought of Peters. Maybe all of us are spiders.

The walls inside are plaster, and we've made no effort

to hide the trowel scars when we painted. One long wall has been muraled by John in primary acrylic colors and bits of glass and tile. She moved over to it immediately and reached a hand out to trace a humpy line.

"Wow."

"John's doing."

"Is it a landscape?"

Of course it was a landscape. I forgave the question after I looked at it with her for a moment. I had seen the sketch on the white wall, and had watched for two months as he added paint and glass shards; I knew what it was only because I had seen him make it.

"In a way it's a landscape," I said. "But it's a bit more than that. It's a star map."

"A *red* star map?"

That's what I'll remember of her, when I'm old. The specifics of my lust will be forgotten, but not the fact that she could calmly accept a star map on somebody's wall if only it weren't red.

"Red's the right color if—" I said, and stopped.

"If you travel the right speeds and look in the right direction?"

Physics secrets are passed on so negligently. "That's not what I was going to say."

"Then, if what?" she asked.

"It's the right color," I said, "if your eye is loaded with it, and John's is."

"Is yours?"

"No." My eye is full of blue. The scarred, shadowed, inside-of-a-hill blue, the color of caverns and pools.

She stepped back and to the side and looked at it from an angle. She'd had art courses, too. "It's quite good," she said.

"I'll tell John you liked it." I never would. I gave it another glance and remembered again why we don't ask people in. "I'll get you that beer."

"Coffee."

"Coffee, then."

She came into the kitchen as I was putting the pot on the stove. "Are the stars in their right places?"

"Let me look." I leaned away from the stove and glanced out the window. "They seem to be."

She pressed her lips together in a funny line: mirth, or exasperation. Probably the last one. "The ones on the wall."

"Oh. I don't know. I suppose they probably aren't."

"I think I'd like to talk to John when he gets back."

"I think everybody would like to talk to John when he gets back," I said under my breath. I don't know whether or not she heard me. "Do you want to see something really good?" I asked, and aloud, on top of my mumbling, it seemed like an indecent invitation from a child molester. Let me show you this, little girl.

"Sure."

John would have my head, I thought. Actually, he'd pack and go. "This way."

I led her out onto the back porch and into the shed we use to store the maps. We have a kiln there, and dozens of shelves, and clay in plastic bags like feed, and the paints, the glazes in mason jars, and John's canvases. In the middle of the room, where we've had to step around it for nearly thirty years, is John's one real sculpture.

"We call it the crash piece," I said, giving away our next-to-last secret.

She didn't move an inch closer. Under the room's one bare bulb, the glass and metal in it glittered and threw the light everywhere at once: into all the corners and into and under the map shelves. "It's the desert," I said.

"I know what it is." Her tone told me I hadn't a hope with her. John might, though.

I wondered how it must be to see it all at once as she was doing, instead of watching it collect in bits and pieces over a lifetime. I hoped it was a revelation. Her mouth opened a little, and I think she forgot I was in the room. I let her look.

The crash piece is roughly square, about four feet on a side. John has built it from what we find around us. My eye goes immediately to a curl of something that looks like aluminum but isn't, half buried by sourwood and cactus. It's a nearly triangular wedge of metal with two jagged sides, wrenched from its whole by its collision with this earth. John and I had followed it one night from its first glimmer in the sky to its burning impact on the desert floor, and we had driven ten miles in the dark to pick it up. There had been a couple of acres of debris that night, but the next morning we couldn't find any of it. We salvaged this one piece and John tucked it into his sculpture. Next to it is a lump of gray glass, a lightning strike, and here and there are odd rocks, and skeletons of the small things that live with us, all towering up from the base in strange humps and mounds that only John's eye could invent and get exactly right. Each time it looks finished to me, John adds to it and it seems more finished.

Caliope took a step forward, and then another, until she was standing over it, and she bent down and touched, lightly, the piece of metal that is central to it. The cactus spines quivered as if alive.

"There's nothing on earth like this," she said, meaning the sculpture.

"No." Buried in it somewhere, too, was another piece of shrapnel that John has saved.

"This should be seen."

"No." I reached out and touched her and held my hand on her shoulder until she turned, shrugging my hand off, to face me. "I need a promise from you," I said. "You can't tell anybody about this. Not John. Not anybody."

"But—"

"Not anybody. If you want to make a friend of John, and have him bring it up, that's your business. But it wasn't mine to show you." It's your girlness that did it, I wanted to shout. My restless hormones. "Can girls be sworn to secrecy?" I hadn't meant to say that; it was a thought that found escape.

"Women," she said.

"Women, then. Can women be sworn to secrecy?"

"I can."

"Then, please, promise me."

She turned away to stare at it, and with her back to me she said very softly, "All right."

"I'll pour you a cup of coffee," I said, and turned toward the kitchen.

"Beer. It's not that I can't make up my mind, it's that my mind keeps changing." She followed me, reluctantly. "Or wine, if you have it."

We have good, solid, well-stuffed furniture in the house, and I heard her sink down gratefully into one of the reclining chairs. I banged around in the kitchen for a minute as if I were searching for the wine I knew we didn't have, and then I opened two beers and brought them in. I sat in the other chair—John's —and tried to make its seat fit mine.

"You can stay the night if you want," I said nonchalantly, without any hope.

"Thanks," she said.

"We have a shower rigged out back, with collected rainwater."

"Oh, that would be wonderful." She shook herself out of her daze and smiled with real happiness.

And while she was showering, I thought, I'd steal her clothes. But while she was showering, a truck pulled up outside and a door slammed. Boots on the porch; not John.

When I went to answer it I found, as I knew I would, one of the young Dinosaur Men whose name I didn't know. He asked politely if I'd seen Caliope. Had she told him she was coming here, I wondered, or had he been out to her place and then come up here through a process of elimination, or had he, as I would have done, been spying on us all afternoon?

"She's in the shower," I said. I'd like to have that moment over a few times. "Cup of coffee or a beer?" I asked. "Out on the porch?"

"Thanks."

I brought the coffee out—pot and all—and we took chairs at the rail.

"I'm not in the way, am I?"

I laughed. "I don't think so."

"I was worried about her."

I nodded. The stars were clear and fine, with no moon. I said so.

It was his turn to nod. "I grew up in cities," he said. "I don't ever want to go back."

"Are you going to hunt dinosaurs all your life?"

"I suppose that's what it is, isn't it?" He lit a cigarette and then offered me one. I shook my head. "I don't know. I like the work. I like the painstakingness of it. My father was a jeweler, and I inherited his hands."

"Bigger clock," I said.

"Yes. That's it." He smoked the cigarette down and didn't know what to do with the butt.

"Throw it over the side," I said.

After a time Caliope came out, dressed in clothes wet from washing them in the shower. Her hair was toweled but still slick-wet, shiny on her forehead and neck. "Hello, Frank."

"Hi, Cal." He made no move to get up.

"I think he's come to give you a lift home," I said.

"If you want one," Frank said.

"Yes, please."

Yes, please. I felt like a dragon; I'd had the damsel chained to the wall and everything. Yes, please.

He took her away apologetically, and I finished the coffee on the porch, wondering how John was getting on, and just exactly where. I put a coat on when it got cold. John would be shivering up on Tooth of Time Ridge. I grew colder and colder as the night dragged on, but I didn't go in. I had done a terrible thing in showing that sculpture to Caliope, and in a silly, childish way, I was punishing myself for it.

5

With the girl bones gone the Dinosaur Men turned to other work, and now, as John had said last night, they were busy slicing open Gonzalitos Mesa.

Six of them were pulling a leg bone from the rock. I know it was a leg bone because I walked up and asked. I'd had every intention of sitting out of sight and watching through the binoculars, but in the end I couldn't resist knowing what they'd found.

"Diceratherium," McIntyre said, and then translated. "Sort of a rhinoceros, with big feet."

McIntyre didn't trust us anymore. If I'd asked a month or so ago, he would have given me a good picture of the beast, its eating and sleeping habits, and the best guesses going on the color of its skin and its sexual playfulness, but John and I had ruined all that.

I left the Dinosaur Men pulling rhinoceroses from the cliff and drove the pickup back for John to take home. He waved from the gully when he heard the engine, but I didn't go down. I walked back to the house to sit in the dark and brood.

It's the way I'd sat and waited for three days for him to come back from Tooth of Time and begin again on his maps. And it was pretty much my job at times like those to sit and watch him. I'd point out an imagined mistake once in a while, so he'd know I was taking an interest, or I'd remark about the clever way he'd pulled up a mesa or fashioned a canyon or imagined a river.

John lets me mix the glazes, and often I paint the maps, and I'm in charge of the kiln. It began because I needed something to do while he was busy, but it turns out I have a better eye for color than he, and I'm lucky in mixing the gray sand of the glazes into pleasing proportions to get the red we want, or the right murky yellow, or the shade between red and purple that's nearly brown, but could never be brown, or is brown, perhaps, to another, uneducated eye.

But right then the glazes didn't need mixing and the kiln was empty and cold, so I simply sat in a canvas-backed director's chair and watched John's fingers stroke the clay. He had the contour maps and our notebooks and his sketches in front of him, but he seems to work mostly from a series of photographs that he keeps in his head.

It was still windy, still hot, but we sat in the shade of Gonzalitos and sipped a good batch of margaritas I'd mixed. The crisis, for the moment, was past, but there were still all the people to get rid of and the surveying discrepancies to figure out, and we hadn't a clue how to do either.

"I was thinking while you were gone that we should get a raft and finally have a look at the caverns," I said. "Survey them, maybe. Make some really, really weird maps."

He ran a thumbnail through the soft clay, duplicating without any apparent effort the course of one of the creeks that flowed out of the Sangre de Cristos. He paused, checked the notebook, pinched out a mistake, and recut the creek's course. "That's a thought," he finally said. "You'd get some weird colors, too."

"You'd go along, then?"

"Sure. What makes you think I wouldn't?"

We've talked about exploring those caves a number of times, and I had the impression we'd never done it because of some reluctance in John, but that was misread apprehension, apparently, on my part.

"Go tomorrow?" I asked.

"Sure." Slowly.

"Live underground for a couple of days?"

He came to a decision. I could see it in his hands and the way he gripped his tiny landscape. "It's a good time for it, don't you think?"

I nodded. "I'll go find a raft, then."

"All right."

"I think we have everything else."

"Bat repellent," he said.

"What's bat repellent?"

"Light." He was right, as usual.

"I'll look around for some good portable floods."

"A couple thousand candlepower, at least."

"It occurs to me," I said, "that we ought to dig one of the old maps out of storage and bore a tunnel under the monkey puzzle with a needle."

"Let's wait and see what happens." He looked up from the creek he was digging just long enough to flick me a light-green gaze; he knew how to time it so the color stayed in the retina's memory after he'd looked away, like the afterimage of a traffic light on a wet highway. That was the end of that.

I took the pickup into Pueblo. If we want something more than groceries, we go there.

The raft was easier to get than I thought. I bought a good, used, four-man inflatable one at the Army-Navy Surplus, and a couple of new paddles. I asked the man to inflate it and let it sit for an hour while I looked around town. I did the necessary grocery shopping, buying frozen plastic meals that would cook up in hot water. We could drop them, bag by bag, into one of the pools.

Finding the lights was more difficult, but I got two hand-held lamps that used large D-cell dry batteries and were fitted into waterproof casings. It amazes me, whenever I leave the desert, how you can get anything you want in even the smallest of American towns, how somebody is hard at work twenty-four hours a day building all sorts of odd things and then shipping them out to the end of the world, where they wait on the shelves like gifts under a Christmas tree.

I drove back home, the raft airless and flat in the pickup's bed, weighted down by a block of wood we keep in the back, its integrity verified. John had put his map up, wrapped in a damp cloth, and was staring at the lump.

"I'll have to finish it tonight if we're going tomorrow," he said. "It'll crack if I don't."

"We can go the day after."

"No. Stoke up the kiln."

In the morning we left our desert's new population to their particular obsessions and drove back out to the caves and walked to the water and those eerie blue shimmering underworld walls.

I flicked a light across the high ceilings and saw them for the first time: what had been empty darkness before in weak lantern light now glittered blue, yellow, red.

"I knew they would look like this," I said, and John winked at me.

We left our lights on them for a while, tracing the arched curves that centuries of flood had pulled away and carried downstream as sand. In our newfound vision, the caves became caverns, opening into an unguessed enormity. This whole mountain range is hollow and would one day fall in on itself, perhaps with the help of an earthquake or a nuclear nudge from all that underground testing. The mountains would shrink to a range of low hills, or sink into canyons, and the river, bottled up, would spring up in lakes.

I found a vein of mica on the ceiling and played the light along it. "Someday they'll discover a use for that," I said, "as an additive in dogfood or toothpaste or bleach, and then they'll mine this place dry."

I shone a light into the pools and watched the bubbles of escaping gas bounce up through the clear, hot water, but we saw none of the feathery-looking, clawed, chitinous blind things I'd half expected, none of the snake-bodied salamanders I remembered from the books. The heat perking from the earth's core would cook them. Against the walls gleamed the red eyes of rats, but in twos, not in dozens.

"I'd forgotten about them," John said. "Sleeping here might be risky."

"We can sleep on the raft," I said. "Anchor it out in the river."

"Rats swim."

"They do?"

He nodded.

I had guessed we could kick them into the river, like little soccer balls, and they'd float big-bellied with the current into Texas.

The river flowed sluggishly from the northwest to the southeast, crossing the range at nearly right angles, and emptied, most likely, into the great Oglalla Aquifer that was buried beneath half a dozen states. Upstream and down it looked navigable, but a bend in each direction made that uncertain.

John pulled the foot pump from his pack and I spread the collapsed raft out on the rock, pulling it square as I would a beach towel. He connected the two, and I set to work on the miniature bellows.

"Which way looks best?" he asked. "Upstream from the start of things, downstream to the end?"

"Up," I said. The boat was beginning to take shape, bellying out, its shiny gray sides filling and shining with its own eerie reflection from the walls.

"Why up?"

"Down, then."

"Up's good. If we get tired, or hurt, we can drift down."

That sounded ominous, but it wouldn't have sounded much more cheerful in the sunlight.

We stowed our gear in the boat and disconnected the foot pump. We had a portable white-gas cooking stove, our foodstuffs, the lights and extra batteries, a complete change of clothes, the sort of rubber waders that fishermen wear, rock hammers, hardhats, two hundred feet of nylon climbing rope, pots for boiling water, and a camper's folding frying pan. We had matches and pencils and our notebooks in little plastic bags, tied closed with twist-ties, packed inside other little plastic bags. We'd both brought knives.

I dragged the raft into the water and John rolled into it while I held on. He had a difficult time getting balanced and comfortable and in the end had to jam a half-loaded pack under his stump as a cushion. I shoved off and climbed into the other seat. We spun lazily. Without discussing it, I became rudder and steering oar, while John stroked.

What is most remarkable is the way the world floats with you; there is only that small circle of light, only the present. What is behind is dark and gone, and what is in front is dark and not yet come. All except the now, the light, is imagination or memory, but no longer or not yet real. I thought the world above in the sun is only fanciful anyway.

We had to make our way around a jumble of rocks in midstream only twice; the ceiling had fallen in such quantities, we guessed, that the river couldn't yet carry it off. There were no other barriers, no rapids or waterfalls (the possibility of waterfalls didn't occur to us until later), only the gentle current and a slow, winding passage that was difficult to keep the shape of in our minds. Curves are illusory unless you have straight lines to judge them by.

In about an hour—it seemed like half a day—the ceiling grew closer, and then dropped closer still until it was directly overhead and threatened to scrape our hardhats. I repositioned my lamp at a forty-five-degree angle to keep an eye on it, as John's was pointing straight ahead, looking for dangers. The mica in the walls was stronger— thicker—reflecting our light like tinfoil. We found ourselves squinting, and my eyes began to ache with this new version of snow blindness.

"We should have brought sunglasses," I said. They were on the truck's dash.

"Who would have thought of that?"

The river was impossibly long. I'd thought if we were lucky, we could travel a mile or two in each direction, but it was beginning to look as if we could travel from ocean to ocean. When we stopped, still surrounded by sheer walls and low ceiling, we estimated we'd gone twenty miles and were deep under the mountains, perhaps on their western flank, but our estimates meant nothing: it might have been two, or half that. Claustrophobia was settling on us like a hand. I began to whisper and pant a bit between words, even though the air was good and a breeze blew in from whatever entrances feed this vacant place.

It was the dark doing it; that, and the millions of tons—unguessable miles—of rock suspended impossibly above us. And the emptiness: we found no gravel beaches at a turn, no hot pools, no human remains or primitive art painted or scratched on the walls, no jewels or gold, none of the treasures that each of us had hatched in his mind. There was nothing but the river and the straight walls of the mountain.

"I wouldn't have thought we could get this far," I said.

"Take out the river and lay down a railroad," John agreed.

We went on for miles more, until John must have been exhausted, but we found no place to duck in and tie the raft up, no place to stretch out and fix something to eat, nothing but the river's beginning that seemingly had been bored through the rock instead of finding its way naturally through slips and cave-ins and mistakes.

"Turn back?" John asked, and I spun the raft around while he was still looking over his shoulder at me. Sometimes the beginnings of things aren't approachable.

When we got back to the hot pools we were tired and hungry and fairly unenthusiastic about taking the river downstream. We threw some plastic-packaged boiler meals into one of the pools and climbed into the others ourselves. The beef stew (I think that's what it was) wasn't cooked through hot when we ate it, but it was warm and chewable, and we washed it down with a large number of cold beers we'd left dangling in the river in a net bag. We slept on the raft, out in the current, anchored with a two-man rock we tied to the climbing rope and heaved in. We should have walked out and slept in the truck, or gone home. I slept fitfully, dreaming of rats scaling the boat's slick gray sides with long knives in their jaws and black patches strung sideways over their red, gleaming eyes.

John, in the morning, looked tired. He has always been round-shouldered anyway, but the years of hauling himself around on his crutches and bending over his meticulously fraudulent maps have made him hunchbacked when he relaxes. I'd noticed this, I guess, from day to day but had never until that morning seen him as others must: a bald, old, sullen-looking man with an odd, misplaced balance. His eyebrows, long since bleached white like mine, were white for real. I wondered when that had happened. Age creeps up slowly, with long, frozen steps, and then pounces like a cat when you blink. He was top-heavy, dart-shaped. He reminded me suddenly of the nib in my grandfather's fountain pen.

"You look like hell," I said to get rid of these poisonous thoughts.

"Same to you." And then he said it with a gesture.

I pulled the toilet paper out of the pack, and after a little discussion we agreed it was best to relieve ourselves in the river. It was a tricky business, balancing on the raft, and not altogether successful. At home, our outhouse is perched on the edge of the cliff, and this was a little like that. I didn't like to think of what accumulates on scree slopes.

"This river needs a name," I said. We were both oddly embarrassed, and I wanted to fill up the quiet. "It's our right as explorers."

"Alph."

"Not anymore," I said.

"Styx, then."

"Is that the one in the—"

"Underworld," he said. "Yes."

"How about something more cheerful? The Merline River, after me."

"The Suope River. It has a better ring."

"Stop it."

We agreed, after a while, not to name it, and that done—a good day's work this early—we had another beer.

"What was the name of that burro we had, the one that wandered off?"

John couldn't remember. We drank and tried to think of it. He had come to us lame and half starved on a New Year's Day morning with ice in his coat and a bullet embedded in his shoulder. His back and flanks were scarred from a lash, and he had one white eye.

"Why do you bring that up now?"

It was probably because I was missing the light and the air and rock under my feet, and I was missing the heat and the gritty wind and the rich red color in late afternoon that gives the Sangre de Cristos their name. Blood of Christ. But what I told John was, "I think my head's empty of names."

John's was, too.

We loved that burro, out of some perversity. He wouldn't let us get any closer to him than it took to set food down or refill his water bucket. He stayed around until the snows melted in March, and then he headed back up into the hills and we never saw him again.

"We could name the river after him, if we could think of it," I said.

We've had a number of pets and animals around the place, among them a goat, two burros, and a hurt hawk. (And John kept a tarantula once for a few months in an empty mayonnaise jar but got rid of it, finally, after repeated requests and a not-so-oblique threat. Spiders don't belong on this planet. Big hairy ones under glass are worse.) Some have gone back to the wild, and some have died with us.

He said, under his breath, "You're a sentimental jackass." I was meant to hear it, so I didn't answer.

We went down the river as we had gone up it, except this time the work was mine, and John steered. I leaned against the paddle once in a while to keep the raft from spinning in the slow circles rafts like to spin in, fending off one of the cliffs from time to time, but mostly drifting in the slow current in our friendly light. I wondered where it would end, and whether we'd ride it all the way to where it emptied into the huge, cavernous middle world of Oglalla Lake.

We didn't. It forced itself into a narrow gorge and dropped ten feet, then narrowed further until we had to pull our arms in and the raft bucked and trembled through a short stretch of white water that we were past before we had time to panic, and then it drifted again into a wide, shallow pond and bumped up against a gravel shelf.

Downstream we could hear the river grumbling as it dropped farther still, and at the edge of our light's beam we could see the ceiling skim the surface, and we knew then that we'd come as far this way as we could, and that this was the end of our short expedition.

"Quite a ride," I said, to say something.

John reached over the side and dug his hand into the gravel to steady the raft. "A better ride is getting back up it again," he said. "We're not going to be able to paddle through those rapids."

We climbed out and slogged up the short beach to a slick patch of rock. I pumped the stove and lit it, and put some river water on to boil. John played the light over the wall behind me, glassy with curtains of water, and the light that bounced back was strong enough to throw shadows.

"So how are we going to get back?" he asked.

For a minute I couldn't think at all, not in pictures or even in words, so I watched the water in the pot. "I don't know yet," I finally said. "Walk it, maybe. It's probably not deep."

John wouldn't be able to balance in that current on his crutches, but there was no need for him to say so. What he'd really been asking was, "How am I going to get back?" but I knew that, and he knew that I knew that, and we both knew that I'd have to go first and take the rope and anchor it to something and pull the raft with him in it. I wished for strength. The only real questions were did I have enough of that and did we have enough rope.

"Making tea?"

I nodded. "Would you rather have another beer?"

"No. I'm freezing."

The rock was wet, and the gravel had sucked at our ankles, filling our boots with cold grit. He poled about with one crutch while the water heated, holding it by its narrow end and dragging piles of gravel from the river's scree slope to him by the triangular, wedge-shaped armpit rocker.

"Why did you bring the old sticks?" I hadn't seen him with wooden crutches in years and hadn't noticed, until now, that the aluminum ones were missing.

"They float."

They also made a nice seine, and soon he had a good-sized mound of loose rock in front of him.

"Are you looking for anything in particular?" I floated two teabags in the hot water I'd made and carefully dipped out two cups.

"Not really." He sifted the gravel through his hands. "Got the frying pan nearby?"

I handed it to him with the tea.

"This is granite and limestone," he said.

"So?"

"And water. At a bend. Gravel shelf."

"That seems about right, John," I said, looking around. "I feel better now, knowing that."

He sipped his tea absently, scooping gravel into the frying pan with his free hand. He swirled it, spilling gravel and water over one edge.

"Gold?" I asked, finally getting it.

"It would be a good place."

"What would we do with it?"

He looked up at me, and in that light his eyes looked yellow. "You don't have to do anything with it," he said. "But we could buy New Mexico and kick everybody out."

"And plant monkey puzzles from horizon to horizon."

"And buy the Foundation."

"And disband it."

"And fire—Ah."

"Fire *who?*"

"Look at this."

I admit I expected him to drop a half-pound nugget into my hand. There isn't a better place for dreams of that sort than a wet rock at the bend of an underground river, but he passed me a seashell.

You can find seashells everywhere, I know: at the tops of mountains and in the middle of deserts, but here, under a mountain range in New Mexico, it was apparent to me as nothing ever has been that this was Nature's shell, brought here in whatever strange manner an unguessable number of years ago. It hadn't been dropped by a child, or a tourist, or a traveler, and it hadn't simply settled at the bottom of a sea into hardening rock, like those turtle shells. It was a gift.

John has added it to the crash piece. It is a broken double spiral of calcified rock (or petrified calcium, I don't know), hollow, open, a swirl of whorls and holes, pitted and rough and weathered, the opposite of what you might expect from something that had spent that much time in sand and water, certainly not the smooth, glassy item it had been when new. I held it and felt lonely.

"It doesn't seem possible," I said.

"Here's another."

The spell, as intense as it was brief, was broken. The shell's value was diminished, and when John handed me a third, a fourth, and then a fifth, I had to force myself to accept them, had to ask myself what we can leave behind that will last half as long. Nothing but the glazed sand a mile deep in the desert, the nuclear glass we keep blowing. I stuck it in my pocket for that reason, and then gave it back to John for his sculpture.

We stayed the night, sleeping curled up in the beached raft to keep dry.

"The thing to do," I told John in the morning—my watch read four o'clock; I guessed it was morning—"is to tie the line to the raft and walk upstream and see how far I get."

I'd hoped he'd come up with something better, but he only nodded. "Wish I could go with you," he said.

"Somebody has to stay with the raft," I said. "If it gets stolen, we're really in trouble."

"Up a creek," he said, and smiled. "I'll stay here and fight if I have to."

I waded in. It was cold but not deep, and not fast. I had the climbing rope hung on one shoulder in big, easy loops, with the lamp tied to the free end and wedged into my armpit. John kept his light on me. I tried to feel the bottom out carefully, but my feet grew numb in a few minutes, and I stumbled along the best I could until I got back to the rapids.

John's light was still strong. It threw my shadow into my own light, which in turn crossed the river's darkness. It was strange to see myself in layers that way, black-light-black-light, as if we are laid down in patterns like sediments in rock and have to find ourselves in a bizarre circumstance like this one in order to realize it.

I needed both hands now, so I untied my lamp and strung it through a bight of line and then ran my belt through its handle. It swung at my hip comfortably.

The climb through the rapids was easier than I'd imagined, and I was soon standing chest-high in cold water in a pool between the rapids and the ten-foot slide we'd come down. My heart felt as if it would seize up. I gave the rope two hard tugs, which told John to climb in and hang on. I wished for a rock to use as a capstan, but there was only me.

I couldn't do it.

"Tie it off!" John yelled, and I waded into the rapids and ran a couple of loops around one of the stones in a couple of half hitches.

He pulled himself up it, leaving the raft to weight the other end. He came through the white water gasping like a spawning salmon at the end of its life, and together we pulled the boat to us.

"Halfway," he said. His teeth were chattering.

I made six false starts with the slide. He didn't say anything when I went under, and he helped me to my feet each time with the same steady, quiet, remarkable strength, and on the seventh effort I kept my footing somehow on that glasslike slope and found myself in quiet water. I had to pull him, this time, as I had no rock to tie the line to, and I managed it, with the grace of desperation or God. He paddled us the rest of the way back to the pools, while I lay in the bow blowing like a tailpipe.

We climbed into the hot pools and changed into dry clothes, then made our way out, but not into sunlight, as I'd expected, but into night. It was midnight, not noon. Although the truck was waiting, the keys in it, we slept at the cave's entrance, liking the heat again (although it was cold), and the stars, and the vast stretches of dark light around us.

"Make it Surveyor," John said.

"What's that?"

"The river. Call it Surveyor."

Something moved in the heavens—a satellite probably—and I closed my eyes and drew in the warmth from the rock under me, and slept peacefully, feeling watched.

6

The past was driving its armies through me. Memory is closer to dream than reality—perhaps it's the bridge between the two—and I was well aware that the events of days or weeks could pack themselves into moments in the mind. Years fell away on themselves and landed in piles. Each chisel gouge of the present exposed the past's vast underpinnings. John drove up to the house with a pickup full of lumber, payment in advance for his new contract with Caliope. I lit a kerosene lamp in the living room, but he'd probably already seen that I'd been sitting in the dark.

There was a god-awful noise outside. He'd need a hand with the wood, I thought, and then remembered his new leg and sat back down and decided to let him shift it himself.

"Need a hand?" I asked anyway, apologizing for something he didn't know about, when he came in a few minutes later.

"No, thanks."

I looked out and saw the lumber neatly stacked by the porch. "How did you manage that?"

"Dropped the tailgate, backed up, and stopped." He slid one palm against the other. "Easy." He glanced into the dark kitchen and then sat in his chair. "Make any dinner?"

"I can."

"I'm beat."

"I'll get some steaks out." Cooking fell to me, mostly. I like to do it, and I'm better at it.

"Expect a visit later from the Dinosaur Men," he said.

"Why's that?"

He shrugged. "Peters came by while I was working and said he'd like to see us."

"That guy gives me the creeps," I said.

"Does he look already dead to you, too?"

I nodded. He looked at you without expression, like a lizard would, as if the desert had sucked the animation from him.

"Have you figured out a way to crate your stuff yet?" I asked from the kitchen, lighting the stove. John hobbled in on his crutches and sat at the table. I looked at his empty hip. "Don't leave it where I'll trip over it," I said.

"It's next to the chair."

"You're supposed to leave it on."

"Can't." He rubbed the stump. "Boxes aren't hard to build," he said, closing that other subject. "Hammer little pieces on the inside and the maps should slide in. I'm not going to take as many of those as I first thought. The paintings'll go all in one box. Maps in two others. The crash piece in a fourth. That's enough."

I carried in a small armload of split alder and stoked the stove. "You going to tell me what it's about?"

"It's your fault, indirectly," he said slowly. "You showed the crash piece to Caliope."

"So she told you."

"Yesterday."

I thought I knew all his looks, but he gave me one I couldn't read. "I wonder why she did that," I said.

"Maybe to see if we keep secrets from each other."

"I guess we do." I put a pan of water on the stove and put a lid on it. "I guess I wanted her to see—"

"I know what you wanted her to see," he said, and spread his hands on the table. "I've wanted to hide that crash piece all these years, Paul. I guess because it is what it is and has that piece of something else in it. I didn't want anybody to know we'd picked up part of a spaceship. I didn't want to join the legions of crazies on this planet and have newspaper reporters stop by to write articles and put my picture next to them."

"I didn't tell her what it is."

"She *knew*. She said, 'Paul showed me your sculpture. Is that really part of a UFO? What happened to the rest of it?'"

"I didn't tell her," I said again.

"All right."

"You don't believe me."

"It's hard to, Paul."

"What did you say to her?"

"I said, 'What makes you think it's a UFO?'"

"And?"

"She just smiled at me. 'Where's the rest of it?' she asked again, and I said there wasn't a rest of it. It's just something we picked up from the desert."

"Her hand went right to it."

"That's what she said." He got up and hopped to the icebox. "You know how you felt when I told you last night I was taking my art to Denver?"

I said yes.

"That's how I felt when Caliope told me you'd shown her the crash piece."

"I'm sorry, John."

He pulled the plug on a beer, cocking his head as if listening to something inside the can. "I'm not mad anymore. I would have shown it to her myself, I think, and might not have asked you first. She gets my blood moving, too." He made it back to the table in one long, graceful glide. "What bothers me is we both define ourselves by that one piece of old junk"—he meant the sculpture, I'm sure, and not the metal in it—"and at our age we shouldn't have to point to something and say, 'There I am.'"

"Especially me." I hadn't built it.

He nodded. "Or me, either. Is that all we've done with our lives?" He looked as if he wanted an answer. "That's about it," I said. "And we know a piece of ground better than anybody except farmers."

"Do we?"

So it was nagging him, too; waking all these dead dinosaurs. The earth moving four feet without asking first. A river we lived on top of that carried seashells and radioactive glass from somewhere to somewhere else.

"So," he said, "if I pack it all up and get it out of here, we'll know."

"We'll know what?"

"If there's anything more to us than that."

And what if there isn't?

"Then you're not leaving?" I asked.

"Not yet."

"Then you might?"

"I met someone, Paul. I don't know yet."

"You met someone?" Your wife tells you she's in love with the golf pro. Your husband, who hates work, works late. I shook my head as if I could clear that thought from it.

"In Denver."

"The week you were at Tooth of Time?"

"No. Last month. When I was gone two days."

"You fell in love in two days?"

"Two minutes. I guess it happens that way sometimes."

"She talked you into the new leg?" I looked around the corner into the living room and saw the butt end of it lying horribly where John had left it.

"Yeah. Sort of. I've wondered for a long time what a new leg would feel like."

"And?"

"It feels like hell."

"So you were up at Tooth of Time last week?"

"Just for the day. Part of a day. Then I drove into Denver to see Lois."

Lois.

"Going to bring her home to meet the family?"

"Paul."

"Sorry." I lifted the lid on the pot to see if the water was boiling, but it wasn't. "Secrets and secrets," I said. But why not? This is a strange friendship, without the usual borders. It's a marriage without sex. We could be brothers, but we're not.

"I wanted to surprise you," he said.

"With Lois?"

"With the leg." He tapped the air where it should have been, and for all I know he still felt the plastic there and maybe even heard the sound it produced. "But you weren't surprised."

"Sure I was."

"Or glad."

"Sure I was."

"Or even much interested one way or the other."

"John—" How was I going to tell him how I'd felt? I don't have that ability. I'd felt jealous, which is something I wasn't ready to admit. It was a confession I couldn't articulate to myself, then, much less to John. Had I really wanted John to consult me about buying his own body parts?

"It's all right."

Maybe in some dark fashion he understood. I remembered the way he'd swung out of the driver's side of the pickup and how the light had hit his head and shoulders and the two aluminum crutches he was holding up triumphantly in one hand. I hadn't understood at all the importance of that until he *walked* around behind the truck and banged into its back bumper. I'd seen the plastic leg sticking out from his shorts and looked back at his face to make sure it was John. Back at the leg. "How are you doing?" I'd said, or something silly, and when he'd showed me how it worked I'd sat there and said, "Uh-huh," the same way I would to a car salesman.

I cut up some potatoes and dropped the quarters into the warm water.

"There's someone at the door," John said, and got up on his crutches.

"Dinosaur Men."

"Yup."

"We don't invite them in."

"Nope."

It was McIntyre and Peters. I brought the hurricane lamp out and waved them to chairs, but they chose to sit on the steps and the rail. We swatted at the bugs drawn to the light. Peters (on the rail) leaned against a porch post and closed his eyes.

"We're going to dig up the monkey puzzle tree," McIntyre said. "There's bound to be a few of her bones still under there; her left foot, and her skull. This time we'll go at it the right way, not tunneling." He left a space for one of us to answer, but we didn't, and after he'd lunged at a couple of mosquitoes to give us enough time, he went on. "If we had her skeleton, we might not have to do it this way. We could send the bones out for dating, and if she's recent we could let the matter rest."

"Let it rest anyway," I said. I knew it was hopeless. "Everybody's bones deserve that."

"Not everybody's. Science has a right to some of them."

"Science doesn't," John said.

He said it in such a way that a schoolyard squabble inevitably followed in my mind: *does too, does not,* and I was a little startled to find McIntyre simply staring at John, with the steady glow of the lantern cutting deep crevices in his face. A glimpse of the future. Peters still had his eyes closed, apparently winning his own argument with McIntyre.

"What have you come here for, McIntyre? Why don't you just go and uproot the damned thing?"

"As I said," he told John, "if we had the bones, we might not have to. We could check her age first."

"I don't have them," John said.

"Perhaps—"

"I don't have them either," I said. They were bubbling in sulphur. I slapped that thought away, killing a mosquito at the same time. A cricket started up under the porch and stopped abruptly, probably regretting his momentary insanity.

"Then that's that." He stood up from his seat on the steps. Peters opened his eyes and leaned forward.

"That's that," John agreed.

"There won't be any trouble, will there?" Peters asked.

"Such as?"

"Oh—" He fluttered his hands as an old woman will, sidestepping a sexual word, not wanting to say it.

"Guns," McIntyre said.

"It's not our tree," John said, and I felt again that I was losing everything, even the things that weren't mine.

They left, unconvinced.

"I've got a present for you," John said, watching their taillights.

"What is it?"

"After dinner." He poled himself inside and I got dinner ready.

He carried a knapsack out when we'd finished eating and laid it across his knee. He dug into it and pulled out a gray ball. He spun it so its empty eye sockets faced me. He reached in with the other hand and held up a jawbone. Embedded in it was a row of flat brown teeth.

"You've been robbing graves."

"Who hasn't?" He took the pack by its strap and squared it in his lap, and then began pulling out, like a cannibal child at a birthday party, fragments of human beings. "I wasn't sure ex-actly what we needed," he said sheepishly. "We'll have to sit down and decide."

"Metatarsals," I said. "Left-foot toe bones. And a girl-sized skull." Yes, please, something in size four. Six-and-a-quarter hat.

"Not the jaw, then?"

"They'd just dig for the rest of it, don't you think?"

He nodded. "Okay. I've got two. Both small."

"How do we know which one's female, if either of them is?"

"It's not a supermarket up there, for God's sake," he said, and then squeezed his eyes shut and shook his head, apologizing.

"I don't know," he said. "It's a bad gamble, whatever we do."

The bones had cost him. "That one," I said, and pointed.

"Good."

"I'll go before dawn and bury it. I know the spot for it."

"It's trickier than that. They know about wear patterns and new edges and a dozen things we'll never think of. What would be best, I think, would be to place it so it tumbles out and maybe falls down a slope and bounces a couple of times. Causes an uproar. Shatters, maybe." He looked to me for approval, but found it in himself before I could give it to him. "They make maps of the bones they find and the places they find them in, and the skull wouldn't fit. It's best if it falls out," he said, and nodded to himself.

"Okay."

"Want me to go up with you?"

"I can do it."

I took the skull and climbed into the pickup. He came to the door. "Make it work," he said, and I stuck up a thumb like an old aviator and drove off. Robbing those graves on Tooth of Time must have been hard; he's slept with them, off and on, for the past twenty years.

The desert around the monkey puzzle was spread out in black and blacker squares. I watched the lights in the Dinosaur camp, and then I looked up at the pale fingernail moon and the thick cloud of stars. The monkey puzzle was black and warm behind me. I picked what I hoped was a good place for a slip, trying to remember how the rest of the skeleton had lain. The rock was loose, scrabbly, and I had a hell of a time boring a hole in it. After three tries I got it done and decided I'd have to get back here first thing and see if it was situated the way I wanted. I wondered, looking at the place I'd buried it, if souls were only philosophy until you begin disturbing them.

I was back at the tree at dawn. John would be hammering boards in a few hours. I sat on a root and waited for McIntyre.

But everybody came. Peters and McIntyre brought the four younger men, Caliope, and the Hitch, and it seemed everybody was armed with shovels and small hammers. They stood at the bottom of Kit Carson and looked at me for a bit, and then, as if by telepathy, began to climb, falling into single file on the narrow path but branching out again into a skirmish line near the top.

"I'd like to ask a favor," I said to Peters when his breathing slowed.

"What is it?"

"Don't pull it down until you have to. Don't pull it down out of spite."

"If we dig around it," Peters said, facing McIntyre and not me, "there'll come a time when it's a danger. The worst thing we could do is let it topple on its own."

"There, then," I said. "Wait until then. I'll help you bring it down when it's dangerous."

I admit they understand the love of strange things at least as well as I. Peters agreed (with a nod from McIntyre), and the six of them set to work. Caliope and the Hitch sat on their heels out of the way, having accomplished what they'd come for, I suppose. Women ignite and defuse arguments simply by being present.

I took up a position in enfilade and dug into the small rucksack I'd brought for my coffee thermos.

Two of the younger men, expert with the long-handled, round-point shovels, righthander and southpaw side by side, a comfortable, familiar team in close quarters, pulled the fill dirt out in nothing flat and mounded it beside them. The other two young ones—Frank one of them—set up screens to sift the rubble for prizes. Peters and McIntyre, I supposed, would wade in with their hammers and brooms and paintbrushes for the small work. They glanced back at me once in a while, and I smiled and nodded and tried to look patient and harmless.

Caliope and the Hitch quickly grew bored. I don't know why they didn't go back to their town. The Dinosaur Men sent them down into the dry riverbed to hunt for anything interesting, but they only stayed at that for about half an hour before they wandered off in larger and larger circles until they revolved around the mesa like tiny, slow-moving moons.

The Dinosaur Men sweated on into the hot part of the morning, but more slowly now; the shovels were laid aside and garden trowels brought out, and the tunnel's shoring was replaced, hammered into the dark sides of the hole. If I'd had any sense, I would have taken that shoring away and burned it when I'd had the chance. Collapsible plastic buckets grew like old-fashioned top hats from a tap on the knee and rubble was dumped onto screens. All of this went on in silence, or near silence, with only an occasional "Watch it," or "Careful, here," to interrupt the scrape of metal and stone.

At eleven they stopped for lunch, and plastic coolers materialized and, from inside them, cold beers. McIntyre politely offered me one, and although I wanted it, I politely refused. He shrugged and gave me a hell-with-you-Jack look, and I guessed that was the end of the politeness. I turned my back on them and searched the desert floor for our satellites, but they had vanished.

After lunch, work was pretty much finished for the day. Beer in the middle of hot weather will do that. It started up again briskly enough, but soon the hammer-strokes lost their rhythms and dropped off until only Peters could be heard working under the tree, and then he, too, stopped and pulled his head out of the hole. It must have been a furnace in there.

They took a short break that stretched into an hour and then was voted into a postponement. The tree was safe for days at this rate, and I made a note to bring enough beer for all of them the next day in case they had the resolve to not bring it themselves. We left the excavation site in a good, mellow mood; McIntyre even raised his hand in good-bye at the bottom. I returned it, and went home.

John had the right idea: leave the desert for a bit until it emptied, go commune with the spirits, or whatever it was he did up in the mountains. Of course, now I knew he sometimes went into town and communed with Lois.

The Dinosaur Men arrived the next day without Caliope or the Hitch. In an hour they were into the spot where I'd buried the skull, but perversely they dug around it, afraid somehow of the very slip I wanted. Their instincts frightened me. I was suddenly convinced that it wasn't instinct at all, that I'd been spied upon and they were all holding back smiles, biting back laughs, and that Peters would any minute drive his hand into the loose stone, pull the skull up, and after only a cursory glance name it for the fraud it was and toss it over his shoulder and down the long drop, where it would break like an eggshell at the bottom. Then they'd grin and pull out saws and chains and drag the monkey puzzle's stump up by its roots.

One of the young ones dislodged the keystone with his foot and started a tiny avalanche, and I saw with delight the grayish-white skull-boulder roll away with the rest of the rock. A hand flashed in—Peters's—grazed it, and knocked it from its course but sent it spinning, nonetheless, down the slope.

Work stopped on the other side of the tree. How did they know? "Got something?" Frank asked.

"Maybe," Peters said.

Hell, yes! I wanted to shout. You've found it! You can all go home! The successful deceit sat smooth and warm in my stomach.

They had indeed gotten it. One of the young men brought it up, all smiles. Peters, frowning, kept sifting through the rubble with his short, square fingers. All around him the mood was one of celebration. McIntyre turned it this way and that, and it passed the first critical tests of his eye: shape, size, weight, color. I thanked God they couldn't put a bone between their teeth to bite it like gold to test its honesty. But Peters was the expert on human bones, and Peters, having given it one quick look, had gone back to running his hands through the dirt.

I told John how it went when he came home that evening.

"We bought some time, nothing more," he said.

In that purchased time the Dinosaur Men ferreted out most of the rest of our secret places.

They found the rock shelter on Rayado, where John and I had watched in our second year here the lights that landed on Esquadrille, across the desert floor. For two nights (this was in 1959) those soft blue lights had floated down and winked out, until there must have been three dozen of them on that flat landing plain; it was a phenomenon of the weather, we thought (very hot, very clear), or part of the annual August Perseid fireworks show of falling stars, but we heard on our next trip into town that the Russians were fooling around in space again (and God knows, America was trying to), so we considered them Russian lights, communist devilment, and then we heard that a device had been detonated that summer, and they became nuclear devilment—who knew how all that would mess up the atmospherics?—but none of that changed what we called them secretly, each to ourselves: visitors. We've grown more accustomed to them over the years, though they show up rarely now, and always in winter, and singly, or in twos, not in the flocks and flights and squadrons of dozens or more, as they used to. More wondrous than the lights themselves is the fact that we've grown accustomed to them. John and I have stood outside the house on winter nights and waved.

The Dinosaur Men have come across, too, the road: a double file of paving blocks, cobbles no bigger than your fist. They're perfectly formed, round-cornered squares, set one after the other for a quarter mile. This road is in the high, trackless desert. It begins nowhere and ends nowhere, and we can't fathom its purpose.

They've seen the Cathedral. It's where I found them after we got away with the skull-in-the-hill trick and they had finished with the rhinoceros bones in Gonzalitos. The Cathedral is a red-rock formation that rises from the floor in six sandstone spires. When you stand at the focus of these pillars and look up, the sky forms a blue, six-pointed star. We call it the Cathedral out of some unfelt Christian upbringing, but of course it's a synagogue. The dishonesty in both of us runs deep.

They were digging when I rattled up in the pickup. McIntyre broke away from the group and came over to lean on the driver's-side mirror, past hostilities forgotten.

"Howdy."

I said hello.

"Is this one of your places, too?"

"How'd you know that?"

"Diplodocus bones." He shook his head, then wiped his forehead with a large red handkerchief. "If I didn't know better I'd swear you guys go around hiding them for us."

"Why would we do that?"

"It doesn't matter," he said. "It's impossible. But it's strange that wherever the two of you spend any time we find something wonderful." He gave me a sly, sideways look as if his suspicions, impossible or not, weren't dead.

"Maybe John and I have dinosaur genes in us."

"Maybe. It's going to make us famous. It's a graveyard we'll be mining for years yet."

Our shenanigans with the Indian's skull, then, had been senseless. John had disturbed ancient graves for nothing. The bulldozers would come, and the crews with their picks and shovels, and John and I would be forced to move as Miami grew into a town and then a city. All this because a couple of thousand dumb, ugly beasts had died in the wrong place a long time ago.

"Are dip lock whatever bones good?"

"Diplodocus," McIntyre said. "Longest known dinosaur. Ninety feet." He was trying to be friendly, I knew.

"Anything on that skull yet?"

"Not yet." He looked back at the others, who were busy on their hands and knees with brushes and brooms. "Peters says it doesn't belong. He says any bone man can tell the difference at a glance, and I agree. I think we'll find that skull to be a couple of hundred years old."

"What's wrong with that?"

"The place where it was found."

"The tree's about that old, isn't it?"

"The tree grew in topsoil, of sorts," McIntyre said. "Bones don't."

"They seem to, around here."

He winked. "Anyway, Peters will dig into that mesa until he finds what he's looking for. I know him."

"Yeah."

"It's true."

"I know it."

"Have you seen Caliope's town?"

"Not lately." I nearly said that John was keeping an eye on that for us, but I didn't. It has occurred to me that John might be helping her build it in order to get it over with sooner and chase them out.

"You ought to go look," McIntyre said. "She borrowed a generator from us and bought a powersaw. It's going up faster than the Colorado silver rush."

How crazy our lives are to others. The Dinosaur Men dug into our desert while Caliope and the Hitch (and John) built on it, while I just watched, taking down the numbers and putting them in my notebooks. Senseless.

"I'll go look," I said. "I'll come back here when you've finished."

"We've got months of work here," he said.

"And then what?"

"Then"—he took his hand off the mirror and turned in a slow circle—"then it depends on where you go next." He backed away from the truck, and I saw him through the dirty windshield corner as he smiled at me. "Come on by the camp some night."

You can count on it, I thought. I went looking for Jamieson. He might want some company, and anyway there's nobody better than an old military man for devising a plan.

7

I came across Jamieson at dusk, shaping his humps of sand. I parked a ways off so I wouldn't accidentally drive across something of his in the near dark. His designs are larger than you'd think possible.

Jamieson is almost seven feet tall, wire-thin, and nearly deaf. He has a back of rubber and spends half his waking hours bent double, building berms in intricate, geometrically balanced patterns. He's a former marine colonel and still wears his rank on the front of his cap.

He spotted me and began making his way over, stepping with exaggerated care over the ropes of sand he'd built.

"Merline," he said when he was in range. He has a soft voice and doesn't care if he hears himself.

I shouted. "Jamieson. Are you winning or losing?"

"Too early to tell. I'll know after the first couple of storms."

We shook hands. Jamieson, too, has seen those soft

blue lights in the night sky, and he says he can tell from the fillings in his teeth that they keep trying to communicate, and he's nearly certain that his work is a product of their own machinations.

He calls them santennas: huge spider webs of desert in Navajo shapes, fitted with lightning rods at strategic locations. Frankensteinian. When lightning strikes, if all goes right, his humps of sand fuse into glass tubes, aligning (he says) the iron filings in them and making crude but powerful conduits. It's up to the others—his word for our visitors—to close the loop somehow, perhaps by dropping into the center of his webs the necessary equipment— radio or laser or whatever—to begin a conversation. There are twelve of these webs in the desert. Some have been nearly completed, and he trots out after a storm and bends double the lightning rods that have accomplished what he wants, and plants new ones in the unglassed sand. It seems no more bizarre or fruitless than our own work.

"There's dinosaur hunters about," I said.

"Thunder?" He looked up. The first few stars were showing.

"Hunters!" I tucked an invisible rifle into my shoulder. "Dinosaur hunters!"

He nodded. "I've seen 'em."

"And girls!"

He nodded again. "Building that empty town." He chuckled and pulled the cap off his head and ran his hand through his thin hair.

"The work going all right?"

He stared intently at me, trying to decipher the sentence, probably, and then nodded.

"Show me?" I asked.

"Sure. Come on." He took a step, then turned back. "Walk where I do."

"Of course," I said, but he had already turned away and was taking those high, long, Tennessee-walker steps of his across his design.

I don't know how he makes them because at ground level the shapes are impossible to discern. But John and I have stood up on high ground and seen the complexity of them and their remarkable symmetry. The sun hits them in much the way that light glows on spider webs, tracing thin, beautiful lines in the air, and so we call them webs, though that might be wrong.

"Here's the beginning of the puzzle," he said, and swept his hand in an arc that looped in on itself. He saw what I couldn't, but I nodded.

Jamieson has it arranged in his mind in three stages: the feeder, the puzzle, and the center. The lines gather power, in his theory, and then twist and buckle toward the middle in some fashion that pleases him.

We walked on, nearly half a mile. "Center," he said, and I nodded again.

"Beautiful."

"What?"

"Beautiful!"

"Yes." He takes no credit. He is the instrument.

"When's the first storm?"

"First storm?"

"When?"

He shoved his hands into his pockets and looked at his shoes. "What's today?"

I looked at my calendar watch but couldn't read it. He lit a match and I turned the watch to him. He read the date. "Twenty-third. September?"

I nodded.

"Nearly a month yet," he said. "Around October sixteenth. But the big one comes Halloween this year."

"Thanks, Colonel."

"Don't put money on it."

"No."

He's only right about fifty percent of the time. Still, in long-term electrical storm predictions, that has to be the same as magic.

"Walk me out?"

"Okay."

He led me back to the truck, and I offered him a lift home, still toying with asking for his help.

"More work to do here yet," he said, and he might very well stay until midnight, or later. He has eyes like an owl's.

In the strange coincidences that have been following me lately, I found room for one more, involving Jamieson, that same night.

"Stop it," John said.

"Stop what?" The night was black, widowed by the moon, and spread carelessly with stars. I don't mumble to myself, not even when I'm alone. I looked sideways at him—he was not a dozen feet from me on the porch—and could see only a wet glimmer at the corner of his eye. Even that might have been my imagination.

"You're thinking about Arlyle," he said. "And the Foundation. And conspiracies."

"You can't know that."

"It's true, isn't it?"

"Yes," I said. "But you can't know it." I had only vague notions of a plot, but John was in it, too.

"You knot up, sort of," John said, "when you think about those things."

"My night vision's better than yours," I said, "and I can't see you—knotted or otherwise. It's too dark."

"Your night vision's not better than mine."

"It is."

John was quiet for a minute. "Can you see that rock?" he asked.

"Yes. Which one?"

"The small one that looks like a squashed baseball, balanced on that flattish one."

"About fifty feet from here?" We were both looking into total darkness, perhaps in different directions.

"Seventy-five," he said.

"Sixty, maybe. What about it?"

"Just behind it—a little to the right—there's an alligator lizard."

"I see it."

"What color are its eyes?"

He probably thought he had me stumped, but I've seen a lizard's eyes at night. "Greenish," I said. "Like yours."

"That owl above it," he said, undaunted, "that's thinking about having it for dinner—"

"You know as well as I that an owl's eyes are gold. They glint silver."

"That's not what I want to know about the owl."

"What, then?"

"This," he said. "When I throw this rock"—he might have one; he might not—"between the lizard and the owl, tell me which moves first, and which way."

"Neither will move," I said. "They'll both freeze."

"Let's try it."

"Okay."

I waited.

"Well?"

"You were right," he said. "But you didn't know you were right until I told you."

"I didn't hear you throw the rock."

"Your hearing's going, Paul. You must be deaf."

"You threw it, did you?"

"Yup. Landed just above the lizard, just below the owl. You didn't see it?"

"It must have been a night rock," I said.

He chuckled. Night rocks had fallen on the house once, on an evening like this one. They'd dropped out of a dark sky without a sound, fifteen or two dozen of them, and we found them only by accident, bringing the lantern out to play cards. Soft, grayish, like lumps of clay. Another one had dropped silently while we watched.

"What the hell?" I'd said.

John had shrugged and picked up a few. "Night rocks," he'd said, and that's the only explanation we ever got.

A town in southern Illinois got a shower of tiny fish when I was growing up. The townspeople shoveled them off the streets and sidewalks and put them in buckets. We studied it in current events. I got no explanation then, either.

"See where your owl was?" I asked.

"Yeah?" He was suspicious.

"About thirty feet to the right, there's a scar on the rock."

"My right, or the owl's right?"

"Your right."

"Yeah," he said. "I got it."

"What shape is it?"

"A z," he said so quickly that I reluctantly gave him the point.

"Okay, your night vision's pretty good."

"Not as good as when I was younger," he said.

"What is?"

"And you're going deaf."

We sat comfortably together, the beers long finished and neither of us wanting to get up for another, and then I realized he'd sidetracked me.

"How do you mean I get all knotted up?"

"You do. Your feet cramp and start tapping."

"My feet don't tap," I said.

"You can't find a place for your hands. Your back gets a hump in it and you bend over. All knotted up," he said.

"You can *hear* that?"

"I can feel it. From over here. You're so wound up you'd snap if I poked you."

He was probably right. Even somebody as harmless as Jamieson was beginning to spook me. After all, he was try-ing to call still another crowd—*others*—into our place. There was work here for dinosaur hunters for a hundred years. Peters had the sort of singlemindedness that would take the whole mesa apart, stone by stone, looking for the skull of the young girl. Caliope's film, with our luck, would attract a cult following, become an event, and in a year or two we'd be up to our necks in crazies from the outside. I had visions of wagon trains and cattle cars of dirty, happy families pouring in and raising a community.

"I saw Jamieson tonight," I told John in an effort to get some of this out in the open.

"It's getting to be that time of year."

"He said the first big storm's due Halloween."

"We'll be ready."

By *we* he meant Caliope and the Hitch and himself, and the false town. "You've gone over to the other side, haven't you?"

"There aren't any sides, Paul."

"Of course there are."

"You're drawing battle lines."

"Yes."

"There's no battle."

"You're the one who asked me not to let the enemy into our camp. Then you joined theirs. You're getting so evened out you've forgotten." It's always been clear to me that there's an us and a them, an outside and an inside, and John, too, had seen the world this way. But he was being won over to a stand of compromise—by Lois, by the leg, by his art, by whatever—a position of reasonableness and equanimity that was fine, probably, for everybody else, but not for us.

"You're going crazy, Paul. The heat's getting you. You're beginning to see plots and enemies where they don't exist."

"Maybe."

"No maybe. We live an abnormal life. You fail to see that."

I wasn't sure if that was a question or not, so I decided not to answer him.

"You need a wife and a home and a job: all the things that anchor us as people and drive the goblins away."

"What about you?"

"I need them, too," he said. "I think maybe my time here is done."

"We've known each other since 1952," I said.

"And hardly anyone else, Paul." He moved in his chair, turning in it to face me. "What is it Jamieson is doing?"

"The same thing."

"What?"

"Building his santennas."

"Why?"

"What do you mean, why? For the same reason he's always done it."

"Why?"

"He wants to contact the others."

"Exactly. He's probably as crazy as they come, Paul. But even so, he's trying to reach out and draw others in. That's natural. That's normal. What you're doing isn't."

"You're saying I'm nuts?"

"You're getting there."

"Nuts to want things the way they were?"

"Yes." He got up and hopped over. The light from the house fell on the leg he carried in one hand. He put his other hand on my shoulder, steadying himself, and steadying me. "Come down to the town with me in the morning and help. We have half a dozen buildings yet to raise."

"Ask me in the morning," I said after a little thought.

He went on in, letting the screen door hit him in the back so it wouldn't bang.

I wondered if Jamieson was at that moment bent over his work, following in the desert the shapes in his mind.

John woke me the next morning before even the desert was gray, and our house, as always, was black. "Paul," he said from my bedroom door.

"What is it?"

"I want you to look at this."

"Turn the light on."

We have electric lights in both bedrooms, the kitchen, and the shed. Those, and the refrigerator, are the only compromises we've made, in the shape of a big construction generator, with technology.

But he lit a lamp and I covered my eyes. "What time is it?"

"Four-thirty."

"What is there to see at four-thirty?"

"I'm not sure. Nothing good."

I took my hand away and got my vision. John was standing in boxer shorts, leaning on his crutches. "Sit down."

He came all the way around and sat at the foot of the bed, farthest from the door. He pulled his stump from under him and arranged it so it pointed at me. "Look."

I'd forgotten its ugliness. It was square, gray, crossed with fine white lines, the bone in it making a tentpole shape in the end of it; that much was normal, I guessed. I squinted.

"Tuck yourself in," I said.

He pulled at the fly of his shorts until it lay closed.

I ducked from under the light and looked closer. I could see black bruises under the skin and a network of red lines running like a road map up to his hip.

"The new leg do this?" I asked.

"Yes."

"That's blood poisoning, John."

"That's what I thought."

"You must have open cuts somewhere."

He rolled over. There were two ragged gashes just under his buttocks.

"That must be a hell of a thing," I said.

"It doesn't fit."

"No foolin'."

"That isn't the worst of it." He got himself upright again. "I've got a phantom leg back. I can even wiggle my toes." He looked at the emptiness that stretched out in front of him on my bed, and he looked at it for so long that I began to believe that I too could see five pink toes squirming. "The whole damn invisible thing weighs a ton and hurts like hell."

"I'll put my clothes on and take you to the hospital."

"I'd rather you didn't." He looked from his toes to me and then back at his toes again. "I'm not in any shape to fight, but I'd rather drive myself in."

"Are you up to it?"

"Yeah."

"Are you sure?"

"I'm sure. I'm not going to pass out or anything. I know where I need to go, what I need to do. Tell Caliope I'm sorry."

"To hell with Caliope."

"I promised to help her. She's already paid me."

"She's got a month yet. If you're not out of here in five minutes I'm going to drive you."

"I'm going."

He got up on his crutches and made his way to the door.

"John."

He turned.

"Call and let me know."

He nodded and went out. I lay listening to him dress, and then he went out of the house without another word and started the truck.

I didn't go down to Caliope's town in the morning. I got my harmonica out and blew into it for a while, making mournful noises instead of music (there's nothing better for that than a harmonica), and I was answered by the elf owls around the place. They've nested in the eaves since our first spring here, ridding the walls of bedewed spiders and the smaller lizards and mice. I made coffee but didn't drink any, straightened the place and did the dishes. I looked under John's bed for a book, but didn't find anything that held my interest. I poked around for most of the early morning and then decided the house needed whitewash, so I went out into the shed and got what we had.

Adobe's only mud; it's good mud that bakes hard, but it's never as good as brick. John and I have talked for years about firing enough brick to do the walls over (now that we have the kiln), but instead we patch them every spring or so and go on. Adobe crumbles as it weathers, and it cracks, but there's a putty compound that we've put on, a bit at a time, that has made the place mostly waterproof.

I walked around the house, brushing the walls with a stiff broom to knock the coarse stuff off, and then I troweled the putty into the cracks. I took a whiskbroom to the windowframes and door molding and slapped the whitewash on with a new, cheap brush (we bought a dozen, once), daubing it into the porous surface and slapping it back and forth in an easy motion. I wouldn't have enough to do the whole job. It flew in white drops, mixed in with my hair and eyelashes, and freckled my arms.

The original divisions between the adobe blocks had long since been obliterated by weather and patching and paint, and the walls now reminded me of old European roads: cobbles worn smooth into a rippling carpet of stone.

I tried to believe, like Tom Sawyer, that it was great fun. I gave the owls a wide berth, blinking back at the huge yellow eyes that looked out from under the eaves at my own, and I knocked down the papery husk of a hornet's nest in a roof corner. I used up the whitewash I had and moved inside.

There's real plaster on the interior walls. We gave it a rough texture with the small trowels when we laid it, and the years of paint have given this, too, a worn-cobbles look. We paint white, inside and out. In the sun's glare, our house hurts the eyes.

I pulled all the furniture into the center of the big room and began on the floors with new varnish. I hate the stink of it, but I put it down slowly, evenly, feeling ahead carefully with my fingers for places that needed sanding or more sweeping before laying the coat on.

I was in the middle of that when I heard steps on the porch. I got up to find Wilkens, one of the ranchers, ready to knock.

"Hello, Wilk."

"Paul. John called me, said to tell you he'll be gone a week, maybe two."

"Thanks. Come in for some coffee."

"No. Can't stay."

"Are you sure? I've got beer cold."

"Can't stay. Thanks just the same."

"I appreciate you coming by."

He nodded, and left. Wilkens was cranky, and I wondered that John had called him. We have other, more congenial neighbors who own phones. Wilkens isn't even the closest.

Now that I was on my feet I could see it was late afternoon. I took a beer out onto the porch. Near the front door a spider was caught in the whitewash, and as I watched a swallow took it, part of an endless high-wire act. Spider legs were left glued to the wall.

In that week John was gone I finished the floors and painted the inside walls (again running out of paint), and when I'd done all I could with the house I walked down to Caliope's town.

The weather was worsening, ahead of Jamieson's prediction. The strong, hot winds would still suddenly, and thunderstorms would try to build mountains of green clouds filled with pea-sized hail. The Dinosaur Men stopped digging and started counting the hill of bones they had pushed up outside the two work tents, sorting them and packing them into boxes, and then they gave that up for a time, as well, and went to work for the girls.

When I offered my muscles in place of John's, nobody objected. We split into pairs and hammered up hotels and dry-goods stores and saloons (she'd changed her mind and wanted an Old West look), trying to beat the rains that could come any day, and while we were at that Caliope and the Hitch slapped on paint and hung signs: Rayado Creek Hotel; Breubaker's Dry Goods; Rayado Creek Livery. She sent a delegation of young Dinosaur Men up to the top of the mesa to build a rock-and-sandbag dam to keep the water back, and I let them go.

I drew Peters as my partner. He was, on closer inspection, older than John and me by about ten years. His cheeks had begun to sag into jowls, and he had the beginnings of turkey wattles at his neck and liver spots on the back of his forearms and hands. Lord, I thought, age is implacable, but it couldn't happen to a nicer guy. I've never tried before to dig my heels in and keep it away from me, but looking at Peters I wanted to.

We had only rough sketches of storefront shapes that had to be drawn freehand on plywood squares, cut, and hammered to the bracing. Most of the detail, Caliope decided, would be added with paint. That had been the original plan, but now she simply needed wood stood up, no matter how unrealistic it looked, before the floods came and knocked down nothing. I suggested she rent a paint sprayer, as long as she already had a generator, and she took one of the Dinosaur Men's Jeeps into town and got one.

The town took shape quickly under this many hands. On the second day we dissolved the awkward pairings and formed an assembly line. Two of the young Dinosaur Men dug post holes; another planted two-by-fours; another manned the saw and cut the plywood into shapes, numbering them so they could be fitted together by still another, and so on. In this way, the shoring up fell to me, and I, at last, after thirty years of other work, could put my bridge-building skills to use. Of course, I'd forgotten them all, but I tied the studs together anyhow with short pieces and rearranged the larger rocks in the creekbed to their best advantage for support.

She had twelve buildings up inside a week, and half of them painted. It began raining every day, in the late afternoons until nearly midnight. The rain was not unpleasant—hard, but warm still—and in one brief burst of electric light the desert leaped forward strangely in blue photographs, Ektachrome stills. The monkey puzzle was once outlined in a blue aura that burned every leaf and ragged splinter of bark onto my mind's plate, a picture I wish John had been nearby to share with me.

The Dinosaur Men turned to with paintbrushes and no longer had need of me, so I sat on the arroyo's edge and watched. Caliope ordered yellow for the trim around the window holes and false doors and for the fancy trim at the roofs. They painted in the mornings, before the rain, when the air was steaming and the hot air dried the work in minutes. Sand blew into the paint in a fine spray. One by one the Dinosaur Men joined me until only the girls were painting, and we watched the young women in their shorts and T-shirts, their long, paint-spattered legs moving up and down the crude ladders we'd hammered together, their arms—yellow-red-blue-black—seemingly unjoined from their shoulders, their wet hair plastered to their necks. And then on the day of John's return, Caliope and the Hitch sat with the rest of us and pronounced it a good job.

From this distance it didn't look like a fake town; it didn't look quite real, either, but that might be because I knew it wasn't, and of course it was empty of people.

Towns, anyway, weren't built in gullies. A hotel, a livery, a dry-goods store, a jail, a saloon on one side; another hotel, another saloon, a blacksmith's, an assayist's office, a church, a barbershop, and a boardinghouse on the other. She'd put up buildings in between on both sides without a determined purpose. I'd scattered hitching posts out front, here and there. A water trough grew out of the ground, and a hand pump. If the weather weren't so nasty, she said, she'd build a couple of horses and a stagecoach. As she said that, thunder rumbled up in the Sangre de Cristos, and John climbed down from the truck.

"When do you shoot it?" he asked her.

"When there's enough water behind the dam."

I said she couldn't arrange that: flash floods happen mostly at night and even in strong weather are unpredictable.

"But there's a reservoir filling behind the dam," she said.

"Want to bet?" John said.

"That mesa's flat," I told her. "The water will find another way down."

Frank disagreed. He'd built it, and in his judgment, the place was low enough to collect a good deal of water. "When the time's right," he said, "we can pull a couple sandbags out and she'll have her flood."

"I've surveyed that mesa," I said. "If this chute's plugged, it'll run off the northeast side."

"It's too high there."

"It's not. It's flat. It only looks high." I turned to John for confirmation.

He nodded, wondering, I knew, why I had let them think otherwise. "He's right," he said. To me, "I'll see you up at the house."

"Wait. You can take me with you."

"All right, but straighten them out first."

"I'll bring the transit in the morning and shoot it for you," I told Caliope. "Maybe there's a way to channel the rainwater toward this end. But be prepared to film it at night."

"I can't. I don't have the lights for it."

"Get some."

She shook her head. "That would ruin everything."

I went back to the house with John, knowing that sooner than I'd expected Caliope and the Hitch and the town would all be gone, and the Dinosaur Men, too, if we were lucky, and the place would be ours again, scoured clean by the storms. Then the blue lights would come back to Esquadrille, and the horse ranchers would come around again to sit and tell stories and drink our beer, and John and I could drive back to the caves for a hot bath without the fear of being followed, and we could look up at the night sky without sharing any of those fixed lights with strangers.

In the morning I climbed up as I'd promised, lugging the transit, with the light, collapsible tripod strapped to my back. I shot the mesa top and thanked God under my breath that it was still flat.

"If you want to channel the water up here," I said, "it'll take a couple thousand sandbags and five hundred hours of labor."

"The dam's useless," Frank said, kicking it.

I nodded.

"Then I can't guarantee a flood?" Caliope asked, pointing below at her town.

"You can't guarantee when."

"Then all that work's wasted?"

"No. The water will come. That creekbed fills every year. You picked a good spot, like we said. You just can't outguess it."

"I'm working against a deadline."

"We all are." I shrugged. "But this one isn't yours to decide." What do they teach, anymore? "What you do is build a hunter's blind at the spot you want, rent some portable floodlights and get them set up so you can turn them on quickly, and then sit back and be patient." I looked up at the overcast sky and gave her an encouraging smile. At least I meant it to be encouraging; it might have been a leer, for all I know. "With this weather this early, you'll get your flood. But be ready: they're not called flash floods for nothing."

The group broke up and wandered around the mesa top. Low spots had filled with water, making shallow, gravel-strewn pools. I looked into one and saw water snails and tiny, darting fish. Where do they come from? Are their instructions locked inside the raindrops?

From up here I could see Caliopeville and the Dinosaur camp. The small town of Miami, ten miles away, looked no more real than the collection of plywood she'd put up. A big truck charged down Highway 25, and the growl of its diesel didn't reach us until it was a glint of aluminum on a curve. The wind died and left us in a silence so complete I could hear the pulse in my neck.

Peters walked over and stood next to me on the rim and looked with me toward Denver. I felt, whenever he was around, the uneasy truce that lay between the Dinosaur Men and us.

He did nothing to ease it. "Where did the two of you get that skull?"

He was a good cop, as I guess he had to be in his line of work. The suddenness of his question, said quietly, pulled an answer from me even as I resisted it.

"John knows a place," I said, and sighed. "An Indian burial ground in the mountains."

Peters nodded, not pleased, not surprised.

"You got the lab report," I said.

"Yes."

"The skull never fooled you."

"Of course not." He faced me, and by doing that exposed his back to a long drop. "The skeleton we took from under the tree is much older. Will you tell me, now, where it is?"

"No."

"I'll take down that monkey puzzle tree this time."

I nodded. "I would, too, if I were you." I backed up a step from him and took myself out of reach of a felony. "But isn't the bigger question why anyone—primitive or modern—would choose to live in such a god awful place?"

"Births are always difficult," Peters said, and left.

I watched him climb down the mesa carefully, each foot placed just so, firmly, before he shifted his weight, as only a cautious man would walk, or an old man, or a drunk.

I went down the same way.

8

I told John our monkey puzzle was doomed.

"Peters?"

"Peters. How'd it go up in Denver?" Last night he'd been too tired to talk and I'd found him asleep on the couch when I had dinner ready.

"I'm getting a new leg," he said.

"You're bullheaded."

"This is a different design. I'll have to use a cane to get around with while I learn to work it."

"Silver-tipped. Gold, doorknob handle?"

"That's the one. A shillelagh. I'll be able to stand around without leaning against the walls."

"And sit at cocktail parties," I said, "without causing a fuss and tripping up the old women with your crutches."

"I'll miss that. Whee! Bang!" he said, and grinned.

"I suggested a new leg once," I said. I had, about twenty years ago.

He grinned again. I hadn't seen John grin twice in one

day since an old Mexican had given us some of his magic mushroom juice. "They used to weigh about thirty pounds, Paul. It was dead weight I didn't want to drag around. I never wanted that, just to look normal. This new one will have gears and pulleys and batteries and will hook up to my back muscles and can damn near walk by itself."

I had a nightmare vision of John trying to go two ways at once and having to stop every couple steps and argue with his leg. "That's great," I said, and tried to sound as if I meant it. I did, of course, if that's what he wanted. But a terrible sadness settled over me: when somebody finds his bones up in the Sangre de Cristos in the next century, or the century after that, there will be aluminum tubes mixed among them, and thin steel wires.

"How's Lois?"

"Fine. Working. She says to invite you to dinner."

"Can she cook?"

"Better than us. There's a green part to her meals, and a white part, and a brown part. Then she throws in another color to make it balance out."

"When does all this happen? The new leg? Dinner with the little woman?"

"Next month. I'm supposed to take it easy for a couple of weeks and bathe this"—he slapped his stump gently—"four times a day in a salt solution. Then they'll fit the leg and keep me around to practice with it for three or four weeks. Sometime in there we'll have you over for dinner."

I leaned back in my chair and looked at his stump in the same way a little boy will if a little girl hikes up her dress. He wanted it so badly all of a sudden.

"She has twenty-eight channels on her TV," John said. "She pulls them in off satellites."

"So that's why we keep putting things up in space."

He grinned a third time. Apocalypse. Three times, and we're all goners.

"Want to see it?"

"The TV?"

"The new leg." He handed me a brochure.

They have a shop that sells those grisly things. Arms and legs and hands and feet in showcases; body parts turned out by factories in Germany, Japan, Korea. So that's what the losers had done, I thought: they'd saved the pieces from the wars we'd won and sold them back to us.

The little pulleys and gears and wires in my own face pulled the necessary levers to make me smile, and then the machinery shut down, and I listened for half an hour about John's new new leg—the marvels it could do!—with that smile stuck in place, but not thinking of his new leg at all.

I looked over his head at the wall, at the bits and pieces of glass he'd glued into fresh plaster, at the desert colors he'd smeared from one corner to the other, and thought again of what he'd been trying to do, and how well he'd succeeded. He'd moved our landscape into the sky and given it an infinite depth. When John ran down, I took a cup of coffee outside and contemplated spending the rest of my life alone. John says we've already done it.

The real stars stretched forever, as they do. The focus of my eyes changed, as it will sometimes, and my balance shifted, so I felt as if I were hung suspended over an endless pool. The size of the sky and the desert suddenly frightened me. If I developed a fear of spaces at this late date, my end would be horrible, gibbering. I had to struggle, fighting panic, and push still one more fear back into that darkness where we keep such things.

I finished my coffee cold, sorry that the meteor showers were done for the year but searching the sky anyway for an airplane's wing lights or a bit of satellite glitter. I looked for any blink or streak across the dark vertical horizon, or for the whistle and flash that might mean one of our space toys had blown apart. I searched the desert floor for a truck's headlights, or camping lanterns and, finding none in all that up and down, felt both frightened and at peace and even more alone.

John had a woman. The two of us were now one each. The geometry of our lives was out of whack; the angles and lines were shifting and making familiar shapes unfamiliar. I began to understand a little bit his amputation.

I opened the door. "I'm going out for a bit," I told John. He waved from the couch.

In the artillery they train men to be forward observers. You need good eyes, and a head for numbers. You sit in a tree, or on a hill, and spot the artillery rounds and call new

azimuths into your walkie-talkie until the shells start dropping where they should. The enemy knows you're there
somewhere, the eyes of the big guns, and they work to
find you. Your life expectancy as an F.O. is about fifteen
minutes after the first round is fired. The grunts have a
point man, a hundred yards or so in front of the squad.
Point or F.O., you're closer to the wrong side than is
healthy, with all your help behind you. I've done both
jobs, and my job now, I figured, was to keep an eye on
them all until I thought up a way to get rid of them. Once
our visitors were gone there would be no need to resurvey
the land: that four-foot difference would melt back into
normalcy, and we could go on. Or that's what I thought. I
had no way of knowing that the desert was changed forever, regardless of what the Dinosaur Men did or where
they went.

I put on point clothes—khakis and my desert boots—
took the binoculars down from the nail in the kitchen,
strung a knife on my belt, and packed a lightweight field
bag. John watched me go as if despairing for my sanity.

The enemy had no idea they were being watched, and
that complacency, of course, is what a spy needs. I
checked on the girls, asleep next to that blind I'd recom-
mended, and then I moved across the desert using dry
creekbeds and dark for cover until I came upon the Dinosaur camp. In a knife fight, facing two opponents, you
always keep one in front of the other, in order to face a single enemy. That was impossible here, with the Dinosaur

camp against Stagecoach Hill, but I got into a place where a twist of the focus knob in the morning would give me both camps, one after the other.

Peters, even at this time of night, was at his bone pile, under a white-gas lantern, sorting through his bone bonanza, weighing and cataloging the parts of long-dead beasts. He had about him a dozen large boxes filled with excelsior. An address I couldn't read was stenciled in black on the side of each. His books were spread out on one of the benches he'd dragged from a work tent, and from time to time he flipped through one of these and then held a bone up to the pages, checking, and then he'd note down a number in his notebook (there was a corresponding number, I knew, inked onto the bone itself) and pack the bone in a box. It was only then that I saw the enormity of the graveyard John and I have lived on top of all these years.

I settled down into the sand, cold, and waited for daylight.

Hammering woke me. Peters was filling boxes mechanically. Two young Dinosaur Men were driving the tops on with eight-penny nails.

It took me ten minutes to move, get some blood into my fingers, and then rub the stiffness from my legs and back. I shifted the focus to the girls, busy with the blind, a cell four feet by four feet by six feet, with seats built into the wall where they could sit knee to knee and wait for the creek to fill. From the lengths of the studs I could tell they were planning a short, slanted roof. Put a swinging door on the front and you'd have an outhouse.

I turned the knob and got Peters. He had another bone crate ready. The sound of the hammer came to me clearly, out of sync with the hammer strokes, so that when the last nail had been driven in and the hammers dropped, the double heartbeat of the nail bounced against the rock behind me. I wondered what sounds I will hear a hammer-stroke after I'm gone, and how long it will take the brain to cool after the heart is still.

I swept the binoculars across the camp, stopping at the two white Jeep Wagoneers, and read, for the first time, their license plates. New Jersey. One of the tent's sides luffed in the wind, and I followed a slack guy wire down to its stake, unsecured in the hard ground. Sloppy.

Peters. Two others. Frank. Two Dinosaur Men missing. Inside one of the tents, perhaps, or out in the desert. Or behind me? Digging more bones, still, or with their glasses trained on mine, marking my movements while I marked theirs?

I panned slowly across the basin, careful to shield the binoculars with a hand from the sun's glint. Nothing moved.

They were inside, I thought, planning—or perform-ing—dark deeds, like an assault on the tree.

Damn. I stood up in a half crouch, knocked the gravel from my knees, and worked my way out of the draw. I hugged the contours until I was out of sight of the camp and the blind and then loped toward Kit Carson. This is where they'd come next.

The wind in the monkey puzzle made its hard leaves clatter. They moved, dark green, nearly black, in metallic crashes against each other, but the tree stood as straight as a fencepost without the give of the willows that spring up in the draws. It was the desert's lightning rod that must, finally, be pushed over.

I climbed it for the first time. Its scaly bark gave my boots a hold, and cut through my khaki pants, and skinned the flesh from my hard hands. The leaves—more stone than leaf—cut me and knocked me about, but I got up into its lower branches and built as it was, firlike, I climbed it as I would a ladder until its top branches sagged under my weight and started me swinging. I unclipped the shoulder strap from my field pack and loosened the double buckles to make it as long as I could and looped it around the tree's bole, securing it again as a lineman will, me to the pole, the bole to me. I brought the glasses up and could make out tiny figures that I knew to be Frank, Caliope, Lucky. I swung them and found Peters at his bones. I could see Miami. Light glittered as it caught windshields and windows in the streets. The town had a flat, burned look, as if it had been painted on a rock, or nailed, like boards, to a fence. This high up, the tree moved in the wind, pushing me gently through an arc of a few degrees. I knew I was behaving strangely.

This high up, I tried not to think of the tunnel dug under its roots.

When nobody had arrived by noon I began to work the puzzle, pushing with gravity against razors. The bark left an acid in my cuts that itched, and the flinty leaves stuck to me and flayed the skin from my legs. I had to tear the sleeves off my shirt and bandage my hands before I climbed all the way down.

I decided to visit the camps I had spied on, and began with Caliope's blind. She'd moved her tent over, and the Hitch's. Inside the blind she had her video camera mounted on a tripod, and the two built-in seats had been upholstered with carpet samples she'd gotten from some place in town. Caliopeville was centered in the blind's one window. I looked through the viewer and saw it was neatly framed: a short bluff on each side, the now muddy creekbed down the middle, the mesa wall behind.

She'd set up two portable generators, each of which fed aluminum scaffolds that held lights. At night the place would look like an illegal runway.

I made my hellos and reached a hand up to tap the outhouse's ceiling. "Waterproof?"

"So far."

"If it gets bad enough, you're both welcome to the porch at our place."

"If it comes down that hard, I'll be at my camera," she said, "but thanks."

"Yeah, thanks," the Hitch said, a bad echo. In any real trouble the Dinosaur camp was closer than our place, and it was no secret they'd be more welcome there. The Hitch had become ghostlike in her time here—browner, sturdier, but still pale in the way Peters was pale. Like him, she had an emptiness of spirit that showed in her eyes. She followed Caliope uncomplainingly and did some of what was asked of her.

I don't know why I invited them up to our porch; the last thing I wanted was these two women—either or both—in or around my house again. It was sex, I decided, not me; not the hope of it (I hadn't any illusions about that) but the chemicals in the blood—long dormant in my case and itching for action—that were stirred by the sight of them in spite of me, and were taking over in a quick, silent coup the least guarded areas: generosity, lust, fantasy. They handed out invitations that they wanted, not I. I'd post guards if I knew how.

She was asking me if I thought the lighting scaffolds would draw lightning.

"Yes," I said, having difficulty for a moment distinguishing between the two.

"What should I do about it?"

"Stay away from them." It sounded rude. Hope Colonel Jamieson's rods pulled the fire. Shoot your movie and go, I wanted to say. Take your crazy film back to UCLA, or wherever, and the Hitch with it, and leave us alone.

The two girls didn't look comfortable together, and I wondered why the Hitch stayed, and why Caliope let her. They were different species. More of us are than anybody would suspect.

I walked over to the Dinosaur camp from the movie set and found it pretty much the way I'd seen it that morning, except Peters's two box builders were out in the desert now, or in town, picking up bones in the one place or boxes in the other. Peters was behind the work tent at a diminished bone pile, sitting bare-chested on a folding canvas camp stool with a huge white rocklike thing between his feet.

"Shoulder bone," he said when he saw me. "From those diplodoci. Here." He motioned toward me. "You can keep it."

I guess he had lots of them. It must have weighed fifty pounds. In it there was a hole—a smooth curve of bone spiraling in—that a leg had once fitted into and been worked by a muscle like a pharmacist's pestle in a mortar. I put my ear to it, but it was too large. I still wonder what far-off ocean I've missed hearing.

"Where's McIntyre?" I asked. The other good part of spying is that once you're suspected, you can do anything.

He smiled, as he often did when I mentioned McIntyre, fueling the suspicion in me that John was right after all and Peters ran things. "In his tent," Peters said. "Sick."

"Sick? Anything serious?"

Peters shrugged. "He won't go to the hospital. He says it's just the flu."

"We don't get the flu here," I said. "The desert boils the little bugs dry. We get bites from just about everything and fever—rarely—from mosquitoes, and rashes from the heat, but no flu."

"Maybe he got it in town," Peters said, and that made me wonder, again, what new microbes were at work in me.

I shook my head, though. "Healthiest damn people in the world live in New Mexico. Except maybe the ones freezing in Finland."

"Still. He has something."

"How long's he been sick?"

"A week or so," said Peters.

"He ought to see a doctor."

Peters just looked at me.

"Can I see him?"

"Sure. Go on in."

"McIntyre?" I said at McIntyre's tent.

"Come on in."

He had a roomy four-man tent, with a single cot. Half was crowded with his things and half empty, as if he were expecting a roommate. Plenty of space for another cot and footlocker. There was enough headroom to stand. The interior walls were orange and well lit, with a battery-powered light hanging from the center pole even though the flap was open. It looked vaguely Arabian.

McIntyre was sitting up in his cot. "What brings you out here?" he asked.

"Peters says you're sick."

"Are you a doctor?"

"No."

"Peters is running around the desert, waving his arms and hollering I'm sick?"

"No."

He uncrossed his legs, put down the book he'd been reading, and swung his feet to the floor. "Then how is it, Mr. Merline, that you're here?"

"I just stopped by," I said. He must have forgotten he'd invited me.

"Neighborly."

"Not entirely." I wished for a place to sit. I must have looked, with my torn clothes and bloody hands, as if I'd only just escaped a bomb, but McIntyre didn't seem to notice. "Actually, I was wondering when all of you are leaving."

"We're at the mercy of the weather. You told Cal, I believe, that this is wetter than usual?"

"Wetter earlier," I said. "November can still be dry. You never know."

"We'll be gone before then." He gave me a weak smile—because it was halfhearted or because he was sick, I couldn't tell. "But we'll be back."

"Oh?"

"We'll be digging here for a decade, getting it all up."

"Good stuff, huh?"

"Bone rich," he said.

"Did every animal who has ever lived in North America come here to die?"

"It surprised us, too."

I stood there awkwardly and then came out with it. "You're not shoving off now, then?"

"What makes you think that?"

"The boxes. Peters is putting everything in boxes."

"It was piling up."

"Yeah." I remembered the shoulder bone he gave me that I'd left outside the tent. "He's starting to give some of it away."

McIntyre looked as if he knew all about it. "What you're really wondering," he said, "is if we're going to go after that skull under the monkey puzzle."

I didn't answer.

"Yes?"

"You said you would. Peters said he would. You said Peters would, whatever."

"And he will. This trip, or in the spring." A shiver took him. He was more pale than he should be in that white light, and his bare knees trembled.

"Chills?"

He nodded.

"You have a high fever with it?"

"I thought you said you're not a doctor."

"Just answer the question."

"High enough."

"Nausea?"

He nodded again and ducked his head, as if the word alone had brought it back.

"Muscle cramps?"

"Yes, yes, yes." He looked up, purple around the eyes. "What have I got?"

I was tempted to invent an incurable disease, and I would have, probably, if I could have decided quickly enough whether or not to make it fatal.

"Probably a swollen ankle," I said.

"I do. I did. I must have twisted it. But the swelling's gone now, nearly."

"So's the scorpion," I said. "You've been sick a week?"

"About that."

"Then you should be over it anytime."

"A scorpion bite?"

"Sting," I said. "Scorpions sting."

"It won't kill me, then? It isn't fatal?"

"Apparently not." Those big ugly black ones can be nasty, though. I'd heard of a child dying from a big one, years ago. They're not around anymore. We've pushed them higher into the hills, where they don't like to be. We'll push them off the planet altogether. "You'll be fine," I told him. "Check your cot or bag before you go to sleep. Tell the others. Shake out your boots"—I picked up one of his—"and your clothes before you put them on. When you pack, check everything carefully. When you unpack, in New Jersey, do the same." I gave his boot a shake.

"I'll tell everyone to check for scorpions," he said, looking down at his ankle, embarrassed. He should be.

"And little brown spiders." I pinched the end of my little finger with my thumb. "The scorpions, too, can be tiny. And clear as glass. But it's a black one that got you."

He nodded.

I turned to go. I turned back. "What are you going to do with all those bones?"

"Some will go to museums," he said. "Some to labs. Some to people here and there—men like Peters—who work on them."

"You've got dozens of boxes," I said. "Hundreds and hundreds of bones. And Peters is out there salting more of them away all the time."

"Some will sit in a basement in Chicago," he said. "Leave me my boot."

I turned it over in my hand, about to drop it. A long-tailed, many-legged black insect fell into my palm. I watched the tail hook and strike. I shook it free with a howl and felt as if my fingers had inflated, were about to burst.

9

An immediate vision-clouding nausea that has its hold in the genitals' roots pulls the pins from your knees. I fell over, tumbling against McIntyre's cot. I held my hand in front of my eyes but couldn't name it, couldn't form the brain's language, even, that would tell me I was hurt and what to do to fix it; I saw pictures of sausages frying, oozing red juices, and of needlenose pliers working a cotter pin loose from a large, greasy bolt. Then the tent spun in a bright orange whirl and disappeared.

A thought lay in my dark head waiting to pounce, and it was this: *McIntyre hadn't told the truth.* I watched several faces bend over me—one of them Peters'—and I tried to sort out the meaning of that: *McIntyre hadn't told the truth.* I searched for the sentences he'd said, now or earlier, looking for lies, but none came.

I was lifted by my armpits and knees, and I felt my bowels loosen.

Don't let go.

"Look at that wrist."

"—doctor."

Don't let go.

"—partner."

"—his house."

"—storage."

Don't let—

"—handbubble."

—go.

"Whew."

Did anyone find the scorpion? Had they said that, or I?

My hand curled around one of Jamieson's lightning rods just as lightning struck. Blue. I felt it burn a hole into my palm and then follow my veins as it would steel wires into my heart. With a bright, sharp, brittle sound, I knew it had turned to glass. Jamieson frowned; I was messing up his design. Moses beckoned. Or was it McIntyre? Caliope swung her hips and, crosshanded, pulled her singlet up over her brown stomach and breasts. The Hitch gave me the finger. Nothing strange about that. Wilkens sighted down an invisible barrel, then cocked his finger and shot me. John lent me his crutches; "I won't be needing them," he said. "Are these yours?" Peters asked, screwing the binoculars into his eyes and then pulling half of them away. Monocle. German scientist.

I had my eyes squeezed shut. My right arm had fossilized. My right foot was crossed over my left, pigeon-toed. I opened my eyes to a delicious darkness, soothing, not pitch black but dusky, quiet. Boxes were stacked around me in orderly coffin shapes.

McIntyre hadn't told the truth. There's no mistaking a scorpion's sting for a twisted ankle. There's no mistaking it even the first time for anything but what it is.

The tent grew lighter, then throbbed with light, and a hum began in my head. Something familiar about the boxes. I stared at the addresses stenciled on their sides and read the Foundation's.

Though it had begun with Arlyle in Maryland, it had grown like a cancer to spread its trouble elsewhere. Its headquarters were now in Chicago (our checks, anyway, were mailed from there), and it had branches like tentacles in Los Angeles, Anchorage, Tampa Bay, Atlanta, Trenton, and Mott, North Dakota. It had international offices in London and Tokyo and another planned for Istanbul. Even though John and I receive a copy of the annual report (we're stockholders), it's a monster we try to ignore.

We have long since stopped dealing with Arlyle about anything and now take our orders (but there never are any orders) from his brother-in-law's cousin, a man we'd met once a dozen years ago by the name of Charles Something III.

I saw in that work tent the shape of the Foundation looming, and I convinced myself that I hadn't been wrong: the faint outline of a plot whose purpose wasn't yet clear would, with patience, make itself known, now that I was on to it.

If the Dinosaur Men failed to dislodge us, the Foundation would send in geologists, mining engineers, painters, anthropologists, botanists, butterfly hunters, ornithologists, soil experts, bug collectors, meteorologists, mountain climbers—the list was endless. They had every university in the world to choose from and all their academic specialties; the Foundation could, if it liked, study us into extinction. They could have recalled us, or stopped our checks, but they knew that we wouldn't have gone. We can live here forever on what we've saved.

Voices outside the tent. A strange one among them, but one I recognized. It didn't belong *here.*

"Mer*line* or Swope?" it asked.

"Merline."

"I'll look in on him later."

Arlyle was here among us.

I went to sleep and woke up at the house, with John bending over my bed.

He thrust his head forward, turtlelike, nearly squinting. "You painted."

"Inside and out," I said.

"And varnished the floor."

"Yes."

"Did you fix the roof, too?"

"Does it need fixing?"

"I don't think so."

"I'll leave that for you, when the time comes," I said. "It will be fun watching you go up the ladder."

"You don't think I could?"

"Sure, you could."

"I'll show you."

"John."

"It's still out by the kiln, isn't it?"

"Skip it."

He pointed his crutches, tipped them, pointed, and was off through the front door. I heard that unique stomp of his on the porch.

We bought a six-foot stepladder years ago but hardly use it. I followed and watched him. He hopped up to it, dropped his right crutch, slung an arm through the slats in the ladder, pivoted, and using the ladder now as one crutch, pushed by me.

"John."

He took it out near one of the porch posts and set it in the dirt, snapping both halves of the ladder open and testing that it didn't rock. He dropped his second crutch and pulled himself up onto the first step.

"Wait until the roof needs fixing," I said.

Those huge arms—as if they belonged to somebody or something else—hoisted him up to the second step, where he transferred his hold to the roof tiles. It was a long reach and as he stretched out I could see his back muscles bunch and relax. He changed his grip.

"John."

He pulled himself up to the third step—the next to last—and cocked his arms, elbows out, ready to push now instead of pull. In one smooth motion he hoisted himself toward the roof but miscalculated the distance (I have the eye for distance) and left himself hanging, unbalanced, his hip not quite seated on the tiles and that short stump of his twisted painfully underneath.

"John." I moved to help, but he raked me with his eyes and I stopped.

He pulled again, grunting, and lifted himself clear of the roof as if he were a gymnast on a pommel horse, and for just a moment he was suspended at the edge of that gentle slope by his hands with all his weight resting on his thick, awkwardly cocked wrists, and I thought he would tumble off, but he righted himself, kicked his stump out with a twist of his waist, and sat heavily, dangling his one leg over the eaves. The elf owls fluttered nervously.

He breathed deeply several times and then said, "I can fix the roof."

"There's a hammer and nails and velvet to take up with you," I said. "And boxes of new tiles."

"I'll throw them up first," he said.

"Okay. I'm convinced."

"I climb those goddamned mesas, don't I?"

"Yes."

"Drive the truck?"

"Yes."

"Hold the gradestick steady for hours when you bend over the transit, using its tripod to rest on?"

"Yes."

"I don't need two legs."

"No."

"I never have," he said. "Even when I had the other one, I didn't need it."

"No," I said. "You lost it on purpose."

"That's right." He glared at me.

"Maybe we're just left with the things we need."

"What I need is a beer."

I brought one for each of us and climbed the ladder. I waited on its top step until he made room for me on the roof.

"You know what I didn't think of?" he asked.

"What's that?"

"Getting down again."

"So I'll bring the dinner up. And your poncho, when it rains."

The tiles were hot and I had to keep shifting, burning my hands, to keep my seat and the backs of my legs from smoking. John sat without moving.

"This roof's too hot," he said, finally. "I'm going down."

"How?"

"Like this." He pushed forward until he was on the lip. His leg didn't reach the top of the ladder. I moved to help, intending to go down and do whatever I had to.

"Leave off," he said, and I did.

I thought he'd pivot on his hands again and dangle and maybe drop all the way to the ground and roll—a parachute jump (that's what I would have done)—but instead he launched out, hoping to clear the ladder. His foot snagged it and brought it down around him in a clattering heap. Either he or the ladder or both of them hit the porch post, shaking the roof.

I looked over the edge. He wasn't moving. I spun around, dangled, dropped. The earth around our house has the give of concrete. I sprained my wrist and twisted an ankle and limped over to him, afraid my anger had killed him.

"Don't touch me."

"Did you break something?"

"Don't touch me," he said again. "Leave me alone."

"Let me get the ladder off you."

"Leave me alone!"

I understood, then, because I heard the words choking him, so I left him and hobbled inside.

I went back out when it got dark. He was in the good chair on the porch, with it tipped back a little, balanced between upright and flat on his back, suspended there by his foot on the porch post. I like to sit with the wall behind me, but John doesn't—he balances, always, on the edge of a broken neck.

"Beer?"

"Sure."

"Do you ever count up how many of these we drink?"

"I try not to," he said.

"Tens of thousands."

"It's the desert. It makes you thirsty."

"No, John. It's us."

"It's a little late to reform."

Our lives are wrong, but he was the one who had told me first. Talking about it wouldn't change us. The rest of time was mapped out like a quartz schist that runs through granite. He knew it, I knew it, and I think Arlyle, too, had known it all those years ago.

"John?"

"I'm here, Paul." He thrust his head forward, turtlelike, nearly squinting. "How do you feel?"

I was in the bedroom.

"You weren't just up on the roof, were you?"

"Take it easy."

"I'm going crazy."

"It's the poison."

"I think Arlyle is here."

"Oh?"

"Down at the Dinosaur camp."

"What makes you think that?"

"I heard him. Outside the tent."

"After you were stung, or before?"

"After."

"Well, you said he was coming. Let's wait and see."

"John, we're alcoholics."

"Rest, Paul."

I closed my eyes.

It seemed harmless at first. This was a lark, an adventure, a sort of summer job. Then we got more serious about it. We surveyed in the rain, the early snows, through all hours and light. Our lips and fingers cracked. John diligently made his meticulous maps, but Arlyle wouldn't accept them; he put us off for years, expanded our surveying area to include three states, and told us to keep at it. The job became a career, an obsession, and then a life's work. I think Arlyle had known the first time he saw us that we wouldn't come back from here, and he had hatched even then the beginnings of a plot that would find its fruition three decades later. Had he taken somebody—Peters or McIntyre—and steered him toward the study of dinosaurs? Had he bounced Caliope on his knee when she was a little girl and given her a camera for her sixth birthday? In one of Chicago's new skyscrapers the Foundation has a war room with Plexiglas battle maps and computerized gimmickry, and in the middle of it is a huge table supporting a detailed (no emphasis) world map, and the two of us are there, plunked down in New Mexico: two small, yellow-headed pins stuck in the middle of the desert with a number or code or name attached: Merline, Suope, Surveyors. The Foundation plots all its agents' moves, and up until now we've been holding an invisible line here, against who can tell what enemy, dug in against all intruders.

I swam up out of nausea to find Caliope sitting at my bedside in one of our kitchen chairs.

"Well?" she said. "I'd hoped for"—she banged her bottom twice into the chair's seat and squirmed—"you know."

She was dressed for the coming winter in a checked flannel shirt and jeans and high-topped desert boots. She bent over and untied them, not just pulling the bows apart but unthreading the laces from the grommets and then pulling those out whole. She undid the buttons of her shirt, and then undid the buttons from her shirt, biting the threads off, and then, with her shirt hanging open, she stood to unbutton the fly of her jeans.

I sat up. I would take her, standing, in the one lit corner near the bed, or perhaps (*and* perhaps) on the floor at the foot of the bed, or on the bed, heaped with pillows, or on its flat, hard, naked mattress, or in a tangle of sheets, or sitting, with her gripping the chair's back, and she knelt, now, on the bed, fully undressed, round, brown, naked, and placed her two warm hands on the sides of my face, ready to begin. I ran my hands down her back and then gripped her, one thumb under each of her lower ribs.

My hands fell away, back to my sides. The only love I've ever had is John's. Caliope brought her hands back from my face. She was dressed, sitting in the chair, and looking concerned.

"You know, I hope you get well," she said, and stood and left.

"John?"

"What is it, Paul?" He was at the doorway.

"Was Caliope just here?"

"About an hour ago," he said. "She sat with you for five minutes, but you weren't making much sense."

"She came all the way up here to see how I was?"

"I think she wanted to see what a scorpion sting looked like," he said. "She missed McIntyre's. Go back to sleep."

In my sleep—and I knew it was sleep, for once—I traveled with John up to Tooth of Time and we carefully replaced the bones he had stolen and then as we stood in a high, cold place the blue lights came back and drifted down as lightly as snow and opened wide doors to us and we walked through them and took comfortable seats in soft round black leather chairs and through the windows stars spun lazily in blue-white whirlpools and the place they took us was nothing at all like the desert and so we asked them to bring us back home.

John carried my breakfast in to me, and when I sat up to eat it I noticed my hand and wrist had been bandaged.

"When did you do this?"

"Yesterday. Eat."

"Has Arlyle been to see us?"

"Not yet."

"Have you been down there?"

"No. Eat." He'd built a plate of scrambled eggs and made juice and coffee. "How are you feeling, Paul?"

"I've been having nightmares."

"You smile a lot in those nightmares."

"Do I?"

He nodded.

"What do you suppose I should do about this?" I waved my bandaged hand. "It's odd that in thirty years we've never before been stung or badly bitten."

"Soak it. Like I do my leg."

Stump, he meant.

"What do you think about packing a lunch and spending the day in the pools?"

"That's probably not a bad thing," he said slowly. "Throw a bag of Epsom salts into each one."

"Check with a doctor?"

"I already have. He said soak it."

We drove a long, circuitous route out of our way by twenty miles so the Dinosaur Men wouldn't see us, and before noon we were easing into the hot pools in the caves. John did pour a bag of salts into each one, and after he'd cut the knot on my bandage I unwound the rest of it with my teeth. There was a hard, round swelling like a bee sting on the fat part of my hand at the bottom of the thumb, and my hand and forearm were twice their normal size.

These pools have been put here for us. I'll never be able to convince anyone of that, and I'll never try, but I know with the knowledge as old as this rock that people and places are meant to come together and that circuits close in the grand design (Jamieson knows this), a switch ticks over (maybe), and lights wink on or off some console. Arlyle knows this, too. There's nothing solitary about a life, especially the one that seems most solitary.

I said as much to John, in different words.

"Maybe."

"You must feel the same way up on Tooth of Time."

"It's not purpose that drives me there, Paul, but the lack of it." The lantern shimmered on his bald head as he turned in his pool to face me in mine. "I'll take you up there soon."

"You've some bones to put back."

"I know. I'm genuinely sorry about that." He ducked his head under and then came up and shook it, splattering me with a fine, warm rain. "What sort of person would find his completeness underground?" he asked. "Besides a dead one?"

"Don't make too much of this. I like this place, is all."

"You're looking for meaning." One of John's accusations.

"Well, sure. Aren't you?"

He shook his head slowly, and I caught it only by accident. "We came out here together because we had nothing better to do," he said. "Nothing more than that. It doesn't add up to an important number in some cosmic equation. *And*," he said, knowing I was about to interrupt him, "there's no conspiracy lurking, no Arlyle down in the Dinosaur camp, no unseen threat that has you in its crosshairs." He stopped speaking, and I could hear the water rippling all around us. "The cosmos is infinite and complicated," he said, more quietly, "but not sentient. Certainly not sinister."

"It is."

"It isn't. You're shaking loose from your reason, Paul. It worries me. You'll end up like Peters, scooped out inside, full of unfillable places."

I lifted my hand out of the hot water and held it in the air. It felt cool inside, with the fever gone from it. "What about God?"

"What about him?"

"I've seen you look him in the face and shudder," I said.

"Not me."

"Thirty-five years ago, on that road in Korea."

"I was looking at my leg, I think."

I had seen into John's skull, for a second, all those years ago, and I knew he was lying now. They had a belief over there that you are responsible for a life once you've accepted the obligation of it, but I didn't push it now. Religion has never been an issue between us.

"Take me up to Tooth of Time tomorrow," I said. "I want to see this place of yours."

"If you want to see some place of mine," he said, "I'll take you to Lois's for dinner."

10

The way it worked was a little strange. John had leg errands to run in Denver, so he gave me the address of the place she worked and told me to meet him there at five. I was supposed to knock around town for a day and not get lost.

I ended up in a bar before noon and spent the day sampling beers. There's brands I'd never heard of. At a quarter to five I gave the address I had to a cabbie and slumped down in the back seat and closed my eyes.

Lois was at work in a travel agency, peering nearsightedly at a computer screen. Her little office was in a shadowed corner, closed off by two glass half walls, and I could see the green script from the screen mirrored in her glasses. The woman John had picked was motherly; she would bring coffee and fluff pillows and pat people's hands.

"Hello," I said, and took a seat at her desk. How had John met her? Had he planned a trip?

She looked up, looked at the bandage on my hand, looked at her watch. "Oh—" She hunted for my name.

"Paul Merline," I said. "John's friend."

"Of course." She took her glasses off. Swept a hand around her hair. "How are you, Paul?"

"Just fine. Is John here? Has he called?"

"No. I expect him any minute." She laid her glasses down carefully in front of her. I suspected that she suspected I would show up and whisk John away, and I could see that she was ready for it. "He's going in for a therapy session tomorrow," she said. And then, with a touch of ownership: "For his new leg."

I nodded. "He showed it to me."

"It's marvelous, isn't it?"

"Marvelous," I agreed. She seemed as proud as if she'd built it herself. But it was war's by-product—surplus, in fact—and I wanted to remind her of that. "Has John told you how he lost the original?"

"Yes. He said you drove the ambulance."

"For a mile or two."

"He told me that as well. You were hurt yourself."

"Did he tell you about Tokyo?"

"Some."

He'd gone through more agony there. Coming to grips with his one-leggedness, for one thing. The surgery and the rehabilitation, for another. "He's gone through lots of therapy," I said, meaning too much, but she knew what I meant.

"It's what he wants," she said. "The new leg." How can you deny him that? her look seemed to say.

He wanted to please Lois, I suspected. I scooted down a little in the chair and tried to appear less threatening. "I don't want to talk him out of it. I don't want to talk him out of anything."

"Well, good." She picked up her glasses by an earpiece and put them on, pulling a fold of gray hair out from around each ear. "I'll just finish this up. John will be along any minute. Feel free to look around."

It was a small, three-desk office. *World-Whirl Travel. The globe is our home.* The world that was their home was pressed flat on one wall in colored plastic squares that erased any recognizable coastlines and made all the continents appear unfinished. Hawaii, I noticed, was half a red square (cut diagonally) in a sea of blue ones. Japan, a string of diagonals, was black. America was a soft green armadillo with its tail hanging down.

I slid a finger along a rack of brochures, arranged alphabetically, and pulled out the one on Korea. I recognized nothing and nowhere in it.

John poled through the front door on his short, light-weight aluminum crutches, the kind with handgrips like you find on bicycles and the curves of padded steel that lock onto the forearms. They were probably more useful to him—with his skill—than a new leg. I remember thinking thoughts like those when we'd driven into Pueblo to watch the moon landing on TV in 1969. *Eagle* had those mechanical arms that it settled on and pulled rocks in with. John swung through the doors without a bump.

"Hi, honey."

"Hi," I said. I looked over my shoulder at Lois and caught her glaring.

"Closing time?"

"In a minute," she said.

"What do you think?" he asked me quietly.

"We didn't get off to a good start," I said.

"You don't get off to a good start with anybody."

I wanted to ask him how he'd met her, but I'd save it for later. I should have asked a long time ago. John was right: I didn't show enough interest in his life. I could end our long friendship right now by saying she seemed to me to be a meddling old bag who had found a rich husband and wasn't about to let him go around with one trouser leg flapping. I may have already ended it.

She collected her purse—square, black, large, functional—and hooked an arm through his and then realized, with some embarrassment, that that wouldn't do. They could stand like that, or they could move and John would pull her arms from her sockets. She turned it into a small, clumsy hug and let him go.

"My car's in the parking garage just around the corner," she said.

"I'll follow in the pickup," I said. John tossed me the keys.

I knew I was in trouble as we began a tour of the residential streets. They were quiet, green, with shady houses tucked into flowered squares of garden and yard. Two boys raced their bicycles in the dusk. An old man, watering his front yard, raised a hand in hello. The houses looked comfortable, well kept, and the lights along the street were coming on, warm spots of yellow. Lois pulled into an empty driveway, and although there was room behind her or beside her for the truck, I parked it at the curb.

I carried John's overnight bag in with me and walked through the front door she held open with the same reluctance I'll have when I walk into the afterlife.

She flipped on lights and the radio. "You boys make yourselves comfortable," she said, and disappeared into one of the back rooms.

John sank into one of two big flowered chairs that guarded a television. I'd thought the dangers were all in the desert; I had to laugh.

"What's funny?"

"Absolutely nothing."

She had photographs on the mantlepiece, and I walked over for a closer look. I turned to John and raised my eyebrows.

"Justin, thirty; Julie, twenty-seven; Todd, twenty-two; Julie's husband, Randy, and their kids, Randy, Jr., and somebody-or-other," John said, ticking them off on his fingers.

"And the guy in the sailor suit?" Squids, we had called them in the army.

"Husband."

"Divorced?"

"Widowed. Some sort of industrial accident that I'm not clear about. Toxic gas or fire or something horrible."

"Recently?"

He gave me a sharp look. "Ten years ago."

I'm just showing an interest, John, I wanted to say. Two oil paintings at either end of the room looked familiar, but I'd never seen them before. I suddenly realized it was John's hand I recognized, not the paintings. "When did you do these?"

"The first time I stayed here."

Introductory offer. "So the TV really gets twenty-eight channels?"

"You bet." He leaned forward and snapped it on and leaned back again. "The controls are around here somewhere."

I looked, not knowing what I was looking for, and John pointed to a little silver cigarette case on the coffee table. I handed it to him and he ran through the channels, stopping four or five seconds at each for me to be appreciative. Half were commercials, half news.

"See anything you like?"

I shook my head. He settled on a news program and turned the volume down to a murmur. "Look out the front windows and tell me what you see, Paul."

The carpet was thick enough that I had trouble walking. In my heavy boots I felt like a farmboy in the Oval Office. She had those white, gauzy curtains that old people and women put up, and I pulled a handful of them aside and looked out. It was nearly dark. Streetlights had come on. A paperboy was walking down the sidewalk, wearing his newspapers like a poncho. As I watched, he threw one toward the house; it dropped on the porch with a soft thud. Living-room lights up and down the block lit the shrubbery and the trunks of trees. Husbands were coming home.

"America," I said.

"You surprise me."

"That's it, isn't it?"

"That's it. That's what's in the paintings."

Lois came in and sat on the arm of John's chair but didn't say anything. John had used our desert colors—reds and browns and a murky blue—but he had painted a new desert I didn't know: cars, streets, bicycles. I thought I recognized the paperboy.

"Very nice," I said, sure that I'd lost him for good.

Lois drove the wedge in over dinner. John was right about that, incidentally: she'd made a brown part and a white part and a green part; the extra color tonight was yellow, fresh corn, and for dessert she served Jell-O with fruit in it, catching all the other colors she'd left out. "Would you like me to cut that for you?" she asked.

I was busy sorting out how to pick up my knife with

that bandage tying my fingers together. "Why do I have this on?" I asked John.

"Because your hand's hurt."

"It's not cut." I picked the steak knife up in my left hand and sliced through the knot. Lois looked at me in horror. "I'll just go take this off," I said. "Excuse me."

She pointed the bathroom out to me, giving me explicit directions so I wouldn't wander into restricted rooms. So I went into the bathroom last, unwinding the bandage as I went and looking into all the dark rooms first. She'd covered the bed in the master bedroom with a flowered, ruffled spread that had to give even John nightmares. I turned on the bathroom light, a wad of bandage in my hand. Naked figures in cheap whorehouse gold reclined in nineteenth-century poses on the chocolate-colored wallpaper. Faucets and towel rings glared in gold plastic. The brown tub was clean; the toilet, too. I shoved the bandage down into a pretty, clean gold wastebasket. I saw my old face in the mirror and knew I didn't belong in any home but mine.

I flexed my hand when I got back to the table. My fingers still felt twice their normal size, felt crowded against each other. They throbbed, impossibly, at different speeds. John took my plate and cut up the meat.

"It must be awful," Lois said. She held a fork up. "Scorpions and all, I mean."

"Awful," I agreed.

She turned to John. "The sooner—" She looked down at her plate and forked up a mess of broccoli.

Is she intentionally clumsy? I tried to see things from her side and decided it required tremendous courage to have me over at all. I gave her a little smile when she next glanced at me, and though I meant it as a peace offering I think she took it as malice. Who could blame her?

John was pleased that we were both uncomfortable. He was keeping score. When Lois seemed ahead on points, he'd bring up something he loved about the desert—its sunsets, for example—and if I seemed to be leading, he'd mention how nice it was for a change to be able to see what it was that we were eating. Maybe it wasn't as cruel as all that; maybe a one-legged man needed this sort of vengeance once in his life. I played along and allowed myself to be tossed off balance.

It's the reason, finally, that I didn't take the truck and go home. We hadn't worked out that particular clumsiness in advance—would I stay?—but when Lois, seeing the predicament, offered me the guest bedroom, and John asked me with his green eyes to stay, I accepted politely.

I heard cars all night on that quiet street and had trouble sleeping. Or maybe it was the two of them in the other bed that bothered me. A strange, three-legged beast growled at me in my dreams.

Lois had already gone when I got up in the morning, and John sat in front of the television with a cup of coffee, watching the early news. Light streamed in through tall windows. Her kitchen looked like a photograph in *Better Homes and Gardens.*

"Sleep well?" he asked.

"Fine. You?"

"Sure."

He turned the news down. I didn't know there was so much of it; every minute of the world's day and night was in a file someplace. No wonder Caliope was doing what she was.

"Get yourself a cup of coffee," he said, and I did.

"So," I said, meaning, let's head back.

"Yeah. Well." He cleared his throat. "I've got to stay here for a while. The old stump"—he slapped it affectionately—"looks healthy enough for them to put the leg on."

"It's final this time, isn't it?"

He looked at me.

"The leg," I said.

"Yes. Pretty much."

"It's what you want?"

"Yes," he said again. "Pretty much."

"You'll still take me up to Tooth of Time?"

"Sure. When I get back. We'll walk up."

"I know where you live."

He smiled at me. "Do you?"

"If you still want me to go through the guesses and add them up, I will."

"Leave it for now."

"What's kept us together all these years, John?"

He said slowly, "A shared life, Paul."

178

I left him sitting in front of the television and drove recklessly through quiet neighborhoods until I was on 25 heading south, and when the traffic thinned to nothing I slowed to a rational speed.

But I didn't go to the house. I tooled through my desert as if it were a construction site I was bankrolling. Caliopeville was finished, and the girls sat around with the Dinosaur Men, waiting for their storm. Bone hunting, too, seemed to have come to the end of its season; boxes were still being filled and stacked. Peters poked through the scrap heaps, turning femurs and scapulas over, holding bone rubble up to the light and tracing with a finger and who knew what purpose the lines of once living matter now turned to stone.

Jamieson was nowhere to be found. The horse ranchers, too, seemed missing, their houses quiet, though I didn't knock on any doors. I found Wilkens sitting on the split-rail fence in front of his house whittling a pipe bowl of apple wood.

The wind was behind me, so I eased up to where he was sitting at an idle, but still he had to duck and close his eyes from the grit and I waited in the truck until it settled.

"How's the hand?" he asked when I got out.

I waved. "Swollen. How'd you hear about it?"

"Those dinosaur fellows. I thought you knew better than to play with strangers."

"I should have." I leaned against a fencepost. "D'you suppose they'll ever leave?"

"Soon. No one in his right mind sits through a winter around here."

"'Cept you and me."

"See, there." He chipped away at the pipe for a minute and then spat. "You could take a gun and run 'em off," he said, "but it's too late for that."

"It's not in my nature," I said.

"Yes, it is."

That surprised me, but he was right: it was only the courage—or the belligerence—that I lacked.

"I've run off quite a few," he said.

"I know."

"I even took a shot at one of those"—he waved a hand into the sky—"once. Two barrels as it went over the house."

"When was this?"

"Ten, twelve years ago."

"What happened?" I knew what had happened.

"Disappeared for a minute. Came back down and blew up in a fireball."

"You shot that thing down?"

He nodded, stopped carving. "It's not something I'm proud of, particularly. Who'd know they'd be so fragile?" He opened his hand. "Like a clay pigeon."

"We've got a piece of it," I said after a minute.

"Is that so? When I looked the next day, it was gone. Wondered for a while if I'd dreamed it."

"What makes you think you didn't?"

He smiled at me, folded the knife, and put the knife and the new pipe in his jacket pocket. "You've got a piece of it, ain't you?"

I smiled back. "You ever live anywhere but here?"

"No. Why?"

"I need someone to tell me this isn't a strange place."

"I've been here all my life," he said. "Dad owned this spread and left it to my brothers and me. Brothers're gone, now." He slipped down from the fence and brushed shavings from his jeans. "But I can't tell you this isn't a strange place." He nodded. He would have tipped his hat if he'd been wearing one. "See you around."

The afternoon had some cold in it, and that evening we got our first real electricity, a week early of Jamieson's prediction. It was a high storm, with most of the lightning playing around in the clouds and not darting down as it does here. I sat on the porch, still excited by it after thirty years. The noise and the light aren't part of it; it's the second before that: those massive collisions that happen invisibly above us.

If John left, I'd have to hire somebody to hold the gradestick, or give up surveying altogether. I could, I suppose, with Arlyle's money, tie into the satellites—global map positioning—and let them do my work for me. I could buy a total station and set up reflectors and shoot an infrared beam at them that would give me distances and elevations more accurately than we can do now. I could pay the Hitch to hold the stick for me and go drooling-crazy over her the next couple of years. The most sensible thing would be to retire and learn John's knack of building maps of the land I already know by heart.

The bare bulb in the shed glimmered dully. I changed it for a new one-hundred-watt one. I pulled a map at random from the racks of them, carried it outside, and threw it down the scree slope behind the outhouse. I must have destroyed half a dozen more of the awkward things before I got tired. I didn't know which parts of our desert I'd thrown away. They cost a month apiece, sometimes more.

Back in the shed I lifted the heaviest thing that came to hand—the potter's wheel John uses to make our plates and cups—and with both arms straining and a thigh to help, I aimed it at the crash piece, remembering again when John had dropped rocks on the busts he'd made of himself, not understanding until now the rage he must have felt at times and the need we have to break free of ourselves.

I hesitated, and once hesitating, put it down. That work wasn't mine.

I brought two-by-fours and plywood in out of the rain and stacked them on the veranda, cut up a few of them and built sawhorses, and began the sketches that I would turn, the next day, into crates for John's art. All of it. I'd box every map and painting and sculpture, and when I had a pickup load I'd drive it into Denver and leave it on Lois's front porch with the newspaper.

The star map on the wall I would keep, because it wasn't boxable and I couldn't bring myself to destroy it and it had been a gift to the house.

It took me three days to use up the lumber. John had been wrong about packing the maps: more than one couldn't fit safely in a box, and the box, in any case, would be too heavy to lift. I built flat cases for them, like drawers in a jeweler's safe, and, after driving into town for hinges, hinged the tops. John's paintings—he had six—fitted easily into one box, and all his sculptures but one got crates of their own.

I didn't know what to do about the crash piece—I couldn't lift it and didn't try—so I left it for him to figure out.

His clothes, his crutches, his books wouldn't take up more than a suitcase, something we don't own. That was all there was of him around the place. When I had it all ready I thought for a minute about shipping the whole lot to the Foundation, in Chicago, and that's when I remembered that Arlyle was here in the desert (how had I forgotten it?), so I drove down to the Dinosaur Camp for a showdown.

"Arlyle who?" McIntyre asked.

"The man you're sending the bones to," I said.

"Haven't seen him. Don't know him."

"I heard him here, outside, the day I was stung."

"We don't have him locked up anywhere. Look around."

"Tell me who it is in Chicago that gets these bones."

"Peters would know."

Peters was sitting outside his tent at a table he'd banged together from Caliope's leftovers. He was laboring over a sketch pad, drawing a bone. It was a remarkable likeness.

"The man in Chicago," he said, "is Charles Bedock III. He's the only connection with the Foundation I have. He came out to the college where I was teaching and enlisted me. He doubled my salary, as a matter of fact."

"I know that name. He signs our checks."

"Then who is this Arlyle?"

"He signs Bedock's checks."

"Haven't met him," Peters said, and bent back over his sketch pad.

It was harder to tell, with Peters, if I was being lied to. Peters had lived much of his life in the university, where lying probably came easier.

"Don't you think it's strange that both of us work for the same man?" I asked him.

"Not really."

I watched him carefully crosshatch some shading along a curve, and the drawn bone was lifted from the page.

"You're good at that."

"Art is a function of my work," he said. "I've been drawing since I was a child."

"I didn't imagine Arlyle's voice."

He put his pencil down and stood up and stretched. "When McIntyre was stung," he said, "he talked for an hour and a half about somebody named Barbara. His conversation with her, as a matter of fact, was a bit embarrassing. When I asked him about it the next day he said she must have been a great-aunt he'd met only once as a child, who had died from some sort of surgical mistake." He picked up the bone and turned it in his hand, looking at it critically, as if he'd drawn the wrong side of it. "It appears that a scorpion—or that particular scorpion—has a hallucinogenic venom. If Arlyle exists at all, perhaps he exists in your head."

"He's real, and you know it."

He stared at me blankly, giving nothing away. "I saved that shoulder bone for you," he said. "You left it here the other day." He pointed at it sitting outside his tent flap.

I bent over and half picked it up, half dragged it, mostly lefthanded, cradling it with my hurt one.

"I'll give you a hand with it."

"It's all right." I took a breath and hoisted it over the side of the truck and into the bed. "Why are you giving this to me?"

He shrugged. "You live on top of these things. You should have one."

"Is the bone hunting over?"

"For now." He walked with me around to the driver's side. "The rest of them are leaving in a week or so."

"The rest of them?"

"I'm staying."

"You're kidding."

He shook his head. "I've a girl to find under your monkey puzzle."

"You can't dig here in the winter. New Mexico winters are *cold*."

"Then I'll dig in the spring."

"You're nuts."

"Give me her bones and I'll go."

I was tempted. What was left of them, I wondered, at the bottom of that pool?

"I don't have them."

He spread his hands, an impasse.

I peeked into McIntyre's tent and found another cot in it. I took the shoulder bone back to the house and left it on the porch, a doorstop. I loaded the pickup with crates and drove into Denver.

It was dark when I got to her house, but they weren't home. They must have gone out to dinner. I unloaded eight maps, the paintings, the two sculptures, then turned around and made the three-hour drive back.

I hoped I wasn't forcing his hand. I hoped this was what he wanted. I hoped he would ask me to come get them again and bring them all home.

11

John drove back into the desert a week later in a new Ford pickup. I stood up on the porch with my hands on the railing, as if that could protect me. He walked only as far as the tailgate, where he stood with his crutches in his armpits, one hand on his new possession.

"Nice rig," I said.

"It's time we had two."

"If you say so. Is it ours?"

"It's mine."

"Uh-huh. Big tires."

"They don't come bigger."

"Lots of chrome."

"It's the deluxe package."

"It snuck into the sports-car line to get painted."

"I told them I wanted the tallest, quickest, shiniest, *reddest* thing on the lot that you could still call a pickup truck. The salesman looked at my bald head and my one leg and almost snickered. But they had this."

"Almost snickered?"

He flexed for me. "He thought better of it. I tell you, Paul, the day's coming when we'll just be old men and the coyotes will get us."

"Let's have a look at the engine," I said, starting down the steps, but John knew what I was doing and why, knew I didn't give a damn about pickup-truck engines, and he waved me back.

"How about a glass of lemonade?"

"I might have a beer or two that's cold."

"I'd rather have lemonade."

"Lois isn't keeping you from drinking, is she?"

He followed me into the kitchen and sat at his usual spot at the table. "Did you stop and think when you left that stuff on the front steps that I'd have trouble moving it?" he asked.

"No."

"Or that somebody might steal it?"

"Did somebody steal it?"

"Or that Lois wouldn't want it in her living room?"

I turned, a lemon in one hand and a knife in the other. "She doesn't want it?"

"It came as a surprise."

"I wasn't trying to make things more difficult. I was trying to help you do what you wanted."

"I'll bet."

The lemonade looked so good when it was finished that I poured two glasses.

"Now I'm rushing her, she says."

"Sorry."

He nodded. That's what he wanted to hear. "I paid a couple of her neighbor kids to haul it all into the garage. I think they broke some of the maps."

Probably not as many as I had, but I didn't say so. I wondered why he hadn't looked to see if they had. "I should have thought," I said. "I guess I was thinking you'd have two legs, or that you'd be home when I got there, or something."

"I don't. I wasn't. You didn't ask."

"Sorry," I said again. I refilled our glasses from the pitcher. "Speaking of the leg?"

"It's not ready. But I've been measured and weighed and prodded and poked and massaged until I'm ready to hit somebody."

"Massaged?"

"Not what you think. Nothing pleasant. Something to do with my back muscles."

"Are you sure this is what you want?"

"I don't know what I want, Paul." He understood the unspoken part of my question, though, because he looked directly at my left leg, as permanent as anything I have.

"How long are you staying?"

"Where?"

"Here."

"You make it sound like visiting."

I didn't need to answer that.

"They strap the leg on Monday," he said.

"When's Monday?"

"This is Tuesday."

"Excuse me."

"I haven't moved out yet."

"Why don't you make up your mind, John? Just say the word and I'll go get all your stuff and make kindling out of all those crates."

"Stop pushing."

I knew my own mind, finally. I had suspected that it would take a cataclysm to break us up, but that wasn't so. John was as vulnerable to the small, steady pressures as any of us. I laid my hand on the table as if to grasp his. "I figured a crack wide enough to make you think of moving out was large enough to *make* you move out."

"I've told you before," he said, "that this isn't anything between us."

"I know. But I don't believe it."

"Believe it. This is about my life, not our friendship."

Those two things were the same for me.

"Let's see what you left in the shed," he said, and got up to go look. I followed him in a minute, after I'd finished my drink.

"The Dinosaur Men were running around like ants when I drove by," he said.

"They're leaving any day now. Except Peters."

"What about Peters?"

"He says he's staying."

"Through the winter?"

"So he says."

"I'll be damned."

"That was my reaction," I said. "I told him he'd freeze to death."

John was balanced in front of the crash piece in such a way that I could tell he hadn't decided whether to move around it or not. "He wants the girl that bad?" he asked.

I nodded, behind his back. "Seems like everybody wants one."

He pivoted. I could see him change his mind about what to say. "If I'm going to crate the rest of this stuff, I'll have to get some more wood or reuse the boxes you made."

"Caliope doesn't have any more. She gave all the extra to the Dinosaur Men."

"We're not broke, Paul. I can buy wood."

"Yeah, or you could wait a week or two and fish it all out of Miami Lake."

"True."

"Fire the kiln up and stack it in here to dry."

"Yes."

"It'll be back to normal around here before too long," I said. "Except for Peters."

"Where's he going to live?"

I shrugged.

"If I leave, you can rent him my room."

"Not a chance; the owls wouldn't have him."

He poled around to the map shelves, and I could see him counting the empty spaces. It wouldn't take much math to figure out I'd broken some. "Feel like a game of chess?" he asked.

"Sure."

"Set up the board. I'll be in in a minute."

His minute was twenty. I set up the board on the porch and laid a ten-dollar bill out next to it that he noticed but chose to ignore. I held two pawns behind my back. He chose my left hand (he always does), got white (I like black), and pushed his queen's pawn out because that opening gives me the most trouble.

We were moving slowly in our third game, having split the first two, when everybody in the desert drove up to see us. The Dinosaur Men clumped up onto the porch and, not bothering to knock, took seats in the chairs or sat on the steps. Peters sat on the rail. Caliope and the Hitch had the back of one of the Jeep Wagoneers open, fishing for something.

"It's a mob," I said. "Get the gun, John."

Wilkens detached himself from a knot of Dinosaur Men. "They're okay," he said. He was drunk.

The girls approached—cautiously, I thought—holding small boxes.

"We brought gifts," McIntyre said. "One for each of you, from all of us." He burped. "Excuse me. All of us meaning the ones you call Dinosaur Men." He laid a hand on his heart and crossed his eyes. "Us."

192

"You guys start drinking with breakfast?"

"Thanks," John said. "That's nice of you." He smiled at McIntyre, then glared at me. "Isn't it, Paul?"

I didn't want a gift. The shoulder bone Peters had given me sat at the end of the porch, under the butt of a Dinosaur Man, heavy as debt. Truce was one thing, but I couldn't manage any sort of new friendship, or even the appearance of one. I'd be like Wilkens soon, keeping a shotgun in the truck.

"Paul?"

I thought that depended on the gift, but I nodded, beaten.

"Oh, and I want to give you this." McIntyre held a brown grocery bag out to John. "We're leaving tomorrow."

John opened the sack and peered into it as a child might for a long minute, then closed it up and passed it over to me.

"Are you still staying?" I asked Peters.

He nodded.

"That's why we're having this party," McIntyre said. "Part of the reason, anyway. We spent the day hammering together his house. Prefab from Pueblo. He's got an outhouse, and a woodstove, a desk, a chair, a cot, a dozen drums of water. A window, a door, a roof."

"This is a barn-raising?"

"A house"—burp—"warming."

"You'll freeze to death," John told Peters.

"Or go nuts," I added. I pictured finding him next year in the middle of April, curled into a spiral like one of his numbered, crated bones, frozen, fossilized, grinning.

"Take care of that, will you?" McIntyre asked John, pointing at the paper bag I still hadn't opened.

"I will, yes. Thank you."

"Time for gifts," McIntyre said, and reached to take the boxes the girls were holding. "Here."

He gave each of us a small wooden box, glued together neatly from two-by-four scraps, with lids that fitted tightly, tongue-in-groove. They had been whittled to fit. I held mine awkwardly, waiting for John to open his.

He got a dragonfly. Not the hollow impression of one, but the full-bodied insect, turned to stone.

The rest of the group had stopped talking, and they all looked at me now; John, too, after he'd nodded and grinned over the bug for a minute, motioned for me to open mine.

In my box was a tiny legged thing—still trapped in the rock—with the familiar tail that arched up and hooked over.

"I guess this is appropriate," I said, and they all laughed good-naturedly. I attacked McIntyre with it, gently. "It's beautiful. Thanks."

I had thought fossils to be enormous things, and I guess I imagined the world to be a larger place, then, like the moon had been, being closer, but this hard little scorpion was the size of my thumb, its forward-reaching crab-like claws no bigger than my little fingernail.

"Thanks," I said again.

John was bent over his dragonfly, holding it sideways to the fading light, but even from this distance I could see the detail of its segmented body and its delicately veined wings. I could even imagine, at that distance in that light, that it was still as iridescent as it had been when it lived. It came to me in that instant that the Dinosaur Men knew our desert better than we: they knew its geology and its long history of mountain-basin-ocean-mountain again, and all the climates it had crawled through, and what had lived here, and they knew, very probably, what would likely grow and live here again. John and I see it for what it is—at least, I thought we did—but they know it for what it has been, and for what it will be.

"Ian," I said, the word awkward in my mouth. He came over. "Has this place"—I spread my hand out—"ever been"—I had to search for a word. He waited. "Lush?" I finally said.

"Oh, yes."

"Jungly?"

"That, too. It had trees and swamps and rivers and lakes and flowers, and all that."

"And it will have again?"

He shrugged, then laughed. "Who knows? Yes, probably, in a long enough time. Mountains wear down. Oceans rise and fall. Climates change and ice creeps down from the poles. It can become anything."

"Thank you."

"It's a good specimen, isn't it?"

He meant the scorpion. "Yes," I said. "Yes, it is."

For those two gifts I liked him quite a lot, and I was ashamed that I'd acted as I had. One of the young Dinosaur Men rattled his beer can at me the same way John does, looking for more. "We've got some more in the house," I said, and went in and brought out what there was—not enough to last five minutes—and a cheer went up from the drunkards on the porch.

"There's probably another case or two in the shed," John said to me, but he said it too loudly. Two of the Dinosaur Men were off before we could stop them.

I tried anyway, loping after them in still one more mistaken effort, and Caliope followed me because she knew what was in the shed and wanted to see what I would do, and the Hitch followed Caliope because that was her job. The other men followed the women, Peters and Wilkens and John on his crutches slowest and last.

I guess this nightmare had to happen: all of the strangers we didn't want in our desert we now had in our home; worse than that: in the shed. They milled about, some of them looking for the beer and the others just looking. McIntyre pushed past Caliope and crouched over the sculpture, searching for fossils.

"Bird bones," he said. "A sheep's tooth." Finding nothing of particular interest, he stood up.

Peters spotted the aluminumlike curl of metal under the cactus quills. "What's that? Part of an aircraft?"

"Yes," John said. It could have been a beer can.

He pulled out a tray. "What are these?"

"Maps."

"Of what?"

I had to forgive the question. Like gangster's accountants, we keep two sets of books, and the desert in some of them isn't recognizable.

"That's what we do," John said.

"Why?"

John and I looked at each other, and I think for the first time in thirty years neither of us knew which of us would speak next or what we'd say. It turned out that neither of us said anything because somebody finally unearthed the beer.

Everybody but Peters and John spilled back outside again, and even before they were gone I could hear the tock of pull tabs and the hiss of escaping beer gas from the warm cans.

Caliope stuck her head in the doorway. "The party's out here."

Peters, looking at our fraudulent maps, waved her away.

So she came back in. "What's up?" When Peters didn't answer, and John didn't answer, she raised an eyebrow at me.

"Peters doesn't like our maps," I told her.

She traced a feature with a fingernail. "Pretty."

Peters, exasperated, pushed it in and pulled out another. "Tell Ian I'd like to speak to him," he said, and, surprisingly, she went without a word. Belatedly, to John, he said, "Do you mind?"

John surprised me, too, by shaking his head.

"You don't mind?" I said.

He put a finger to his lips and winked. "Shh."

I've tried to make sense of that since. He suspected what was coming, I think, and he meant it to be his parting gift.

McIntyre followed Caliope in, brushing at his cheek, trying to wipe foam flecks from the wrong side of his mouth. "What is it, Clay?"

"Have you seen these?"

He glanced at the map and shook his head.

"Assume for a moment," Peters said, "that it's a map of this terrain."

What do you mean *assume*, I was about to say, but John stopped me again with that finger to his lips.

"Not in this era," McIntyre said. "Not—" And then, "Oh."

"What is it?" Caliope asked.

Yes, what? They ignored both of us.

"How—" McIntyre began, but Peters interrupted.

"How," Peters asked, "do the two of you decide where to plant a monument?"

John gave me the go-ahead look. "We started with a known benchmark," I said, "and then we picked the monkey puzzle."

"Why?"

I shrugged and looked at John. "We had to start somewhere," I said.

"And after that?"

"I don't know. It's in our notebooks."

"We look at the ground," John said. "We decide on a place and go there."

"Will you do that for us tomorrow? We can start at the girls' town."

John smiled. "Sure. Now let's go back outside and drink the beer." To me, and the question I wanted to ask, he said, "Wait until tomorrow."

The party was a step away from finished. Wilkens wanted to dance with the Hitch, who had lost or undone the top buttons of her shirt. Her eyes were vacant, and her hips, when she walked, seemed unstuck. He leaned forward to hug her into a waltz step—she stepped sideways—and he kept leaning right down to the floor.

She took off her shirt and jeans and threw them to one of the Dinosaur Men and scuttled down the steps and then down into the dark wash, singing, "Whee." The last we saw of her was a pair of white panties bobbing drunkenly and happily about. Caliope went after her but was losing ground. We never did find her.

"I guess that's that," Peters said.

The party followed the girls, of course, back to the Dinosaur camp. They left an empty keg rolling against the legs of an unconscious Wilkens and the debris of beer cans ankle deep on the porch.

The next day the desert looked new. We get our share of glorious days like these, but not very often this late in the year. The rock was red, the sky blue, the heat gentle. As if drawn by a hand, a clear line separated every rock and color, and the horizon seemed close enough to touch. Every inch of this place had been engraved on the backs of my eyes, I thought, but at every turn I found a new blue vein of clay or a hat-shaped cleft in a ridge or another of a dozen small surprises.

Peters and McIntyre met us where they said they would and asked us to pick a spot. "Read from any monument you've ever planted," he said.

John chose a place. "Set up here," he said to me.

I pulled out the transit and leveled it with the built-in carpenter's bubble. I dropped the plumb and watched it swing. The actions are mechanical, now, certain. Drop the knotted plumb bob. Run an imaginary line through the midpoint (just there, that small hillock near the tree). Wait until the yardstick inches into the crosshairs. Make a fist. Read the number. Note it down. Wave him off. It's a simple semaphore.

John waved, and I trained the glass on him. McIntyre and Peters had picked a sterile piece of ground. Four feet and twenty-one hundredths. I waved him off. I wrote the number down, walked over to him, and added it to the one etched in the monument at his feet. He looked over my shoulder at what I'd written. "That's wrong," he said.

"Of course it's wrong. We haven't shot anything right in months. Maybe years." Maybe ever.

John looked over at the dry riverbed a hundred feet away, and I remembered, as he must have, how we'd followed it all one summer, planting monuments a chain away because it never filled and John thought it had to do with the slope.

"So?"

"So, the transit's out of whack," he said. "It's not the desert that needs fixing, it's the instrument."

"I haven't dropped it."

"It doesn't matter."

"We had it checked this summer, before the place filled up."

"It doesn't matter. It's off."

"It's nearly new."

"It's off."

I shook my head. "It can't be."

"What is it with you?" he asked. "Would you rather believe that somehow everything's shifted? What kind of science do you live by? The desert doesn't move, Paul. Not like that."

"Are you sure?" I pointed to where Peters and McIntyre were now on their knees, digging. Peters held something up in one hand.

It was a long skull. It meant nothing to us. We didn't ask Peters to guess its origins. We knew if the Dinosaur Men stayed much longer they'd turn up the missing link or the oldest art of the bones of Adam. "We've got to get rid of them," I told John, and John said, "You'll never be able to."

In something as vivid as a dream I saw hundreds of creatures heaving around under our feet for thirty years, playing a macabre game of musical chairs, finding and dying in new spots each day, and the picture I once had of beetles crawling through bat crap came back with a force that made my knees weak.

We sat down a hundred yards or so from them and watched as their newest excavation took shape. They laid out a grid with string and long corkscrewed eye bolts, and under Peters's direction began to dig. I watched them through the glass, and something about their methods—the way they broke into the rock gently with sharp picks, brushed the debris aside with stiff brooms, and then cracked into the rock again—made me think of weather.

"They're eroding it," I said.

They pulled the desert back a couple of inches at a time, exposing a thousand years an hour, going down a foot or a foot and a half and then moving over to another square. Shouts arose as they got a long bone—arm or leg or rib.

We were sitting in shadow with our backs against a wall of old stone that crumbled as we moved against it. I'd carried the instrument out of the sun, and I watched now as the plumb bob swayed at the end of its long red string. It spun lazily when it should have been still. I reached under the plumb, hating the thought inside me, and dug into the broken rock that had fallen away. I opened my fist to see a tooth the shape of a shark's in my palm. The plumb circled slower, slower, and then stopped.

I turned to John, and found him watching me.

"I don't believe it," he said.

"It's true." I plucked the hot brass bob from its string and buried it in the hole I'd drawn the tooth from. And just like that, it all stopped. The Dinosaur Men pulled nothing more out of the ground.

12

I put the transit in its box and the box in the bed and brushed the dirt from my knees and seat before I got into John's new pickup. I'd never had a chair fit me so well. "This is too nice for desert work," I told him.

"I know."

At the house he left the engine running. "Wait here," he said.

He came out with the paper bag McIntyre had given him the night before and the knapsack he carries on trips. He handed them both to me and put the truck in gear.

I opened the bag and looked in. It was the girl's skull John had stolen. "Tooth of Time?" I asked.

He nodded. "I should have taken the other bones back long ago. Now we have all of them."

"Shouldn't we take a shovel?"

He shook his head.

Tooth of Time is John's territory, and I've never intruded there. He drove through the foothills, following paths only he could see, and I wondered how he'd done it before we got the four-wheel drive. This wasn't mesa, wasn't butte, but one knobbly vertebra of Sangre de Cristo spine poking out onto the pan. In the early afternoon the hills were the color of orange peel without the dimpled, golfball shine, and they rose in humps higher and higher until they finally rose high enough to be mountains.

"Gets a bit rough here," John said, and the pickup obligingly bucked a couple of times and then settled into a sway as John rolled first the right-side and then the left-side wheels into ruts.

"Are we staying the night?"

"No."

So that, at least, was still reserved for him. I felt privileged, all the same, and held the bag on my lap, cradling the skull in it with both hands. The truck jumped a boulder, and we both knocked our heads against the roof.

"Damn," John said. "I'm never ready for that, even when I think I am." He turned the key off and we listened to the engine cool. "We walk from here."

"I'm ready."

He smiled at me by lifting his upper lip on the side closest to me and baring his teeth. "Okay."

I stayed behind him, of course, as he knew the way, expecting a leisurely climb, but John, on crutches, winded me. I thought of that lunar lander again as I watched him maneuver through the rocks, twice storing both crutches through the waistband of his trousers and the empty, cutoff trouser leg and pulling himself up by hand. It was a good hour before he stopped and I came up beside him breathing hard.

"Halfway," he said. "How are you doing?"

"Fine."

"Liar."

"We should have gotten an earlier start."

"The rest is easy," he said.

We've climbed mesas together tens of dozens of times (though it had taken me years, sometimes, to find a way up that we both could manage), but here the footing was treacherous although the slope was easy; the way was strewn with loose rock that rattled like marbles from under our feet.

We climbed to the military ridge, one contour down from the real one, and turned with the mountain's grain and walked easily.

"That shadow"—he pointed—"where the two hills fold in is it."

"Is there water?"

"Beer, too."

"You've got beer up here?"

"You said it yourself, Paul: we've always got beer."

I had a treehouse as a kid where I stored comic books and girlie books—well, parts of Sears and Roebuck catalogs—and other kid treasures, and I imagined now something of the sort for John: a rocky fort with a refrigerator and a television and a big, overstuffed easy chair the neighbor had thrown out, and maybe an art book and a couple of magazines to leaf through on long late afternoons. John's camp, though, was a flat granite slab that sloped down to a fine gray sand beach and into a deep mountain pool. He fished around in it and brought up two beers.

I put the can down unopened and ducked my head in the water. It was delicious. The water crept in under the skin at my hairline just as if the two don't completely join and then worked its way down inside my spine and settled in—filled—my scrotum.

I brought my head up just before I would have drowned and joined John on the slab. There was desert I hadn't seen in years spread out on the other side of the ridge.

"The Indians brought their dead up that way," he said, "from the other side. Much easier than the way we came."

"Couldn't we have driven around," I asked, "and done the same thing?"

"Nope."

I didn't know about that.

"See there?" He pointed at a distant horizon that slowly took on red-brown shapes. Peaks. Rows of them, each darker than the one in front, like files of sharks' teeth. The farthest row glinted. "Snow," John said, and I understood a part of what made this place special to him in the summers. "That's our boundary," he said, "no matter what the Foundation thinks."

We drank four beers each, and the day and its shadows grew too long to go back.

"I guess we can wrap ourselves in the shelterhalf," I said, "but it's going to be *cold*. I'm for trying to get back in the dark."

"Why do you think I keep a shelterhalf here? There's a lot of mesquite along that way," he said, and showed me. "Collect an armload or three, why don't you?"

When I brought a good pile of it back, John had scooped a pit from the sand. He laid the wood in it and lit it.

"If we sleep next to that," I said, "we'll roll right in."

"We sleep on top of it."

That's what we eventually did. John banked the fire carefully with sand and we spread the shelterhalf on top. It warmed us all night. But for a long time first we fed it, getting it furnace-hot. The mesquite broke into small square coals and sent up sparks that danced in their own updraft and fell back on us as cold grains of soot.

"You've done this before."

"Many times. And others before me. There's layers of old fires in it."

"You don't have any food put aside, do you?"

"No." He looked into the fire. "I ate a lizard once, just to see what it was like. Mostly I don't bring food up here with me."

It was hard to find the right distance from the fire. Too hot, or too cold. "What's the elevation here?"

"Eight thousand feet."

"Give or take what?"

"Give or take nothing. It's eight thousand feet."

The sparks died and the coalbed glowed. The Foundation seemed half a continent away, again, where it belonged. The Dinosaur Men shed their cloaks and dropped their daggers, and the dangers, plots, and intrigues of the past month went up with the smoke.

"How far away are they?"

"Who?"

"The Indians, in this cemetery of yours."

"Not far." He tucked a plug of tobacco into his cheek and passed the bag to me. "We'll go in the morning. It's fairly creepy at night."

"It couldn't be," I said, feeling warm.

"It is."

We curled into the shelterhalf on that warm sand, sleeping back to back, but I was awake before dawn, rested, quiet, and wondering, as you do sometimes, whether I'd slept at all. John, too, was awake, and we turned over on our backs and looked up at the still bright stars spread in glittering millions. I hunted for and found Scorpio low on the western rim.

"Sleep good?"

I told him I thought I hadn't slept at all.

"Tired?"

"No. Cold, though." I rolled off the shelterhalf and pulled it up, burrowing into the sand beneath it for more warmth. John joined me underneath it; cold, too, or companionable.

We were both looking at the same square of sky when one of the fixed stars became unfixed, darted down, and drew a letter in the dark—a Greek-looking thing with a long loop and tail—before hiding in the stars again.

Neither of us wanted to say anything in case the other hadn't seen it, even though we've witnessed those lights many times. Why do I have this fear of being disbelieved, even with John?

"It's good to have them back," John said finally.

"If they ever left." Sometimes I can't shake the feeling that we're the visitors here, just taking care of the place for the owners.

The sun came up, a violet, flattened ball, and we knew the day would be hot. We had a beer before breakfast (not the first time for that), and then John led me along a path over the ridge that dropped into a cleft. In it skeletons were arranged in niches like manikins in a store window. Some had skin pulled tight against skull and pelvis, mummified in the dry heat, while others—the older ones, John said—were Halloween arrangements of tied-together sticks, precariously balanced.

"Do you ever see ghosts?"

John shook his head. "This is a good place." He shrugged off the knapsack, set it on the ground, and opened the flap. He pulled the bones out, one by one, and put them back, gently, where they belonged. He took the skull from me and set it in its niche. "Bury me here when it's my turn," he said.

"I will." I resolved right then to outlive him.

When he was done we went back down again, neither of us speaking, John probably thinking, as I was, about death. We've seen so little of it out here until the Dinosaur Men showed us that we've lived our lives on top of it. Now, suddenly, I had the spooky feeling that it was reaching up for us through the rock, chilling my feet. I stumbled.

"Careful," John said.

"You bet."

The next morning was the one day each year that sepa-rates summer from winter, and we always knew the snow wouldn't be long in coming. It dawns, always, very clear and windless, so calm it seems as if the world has stopped spinning, and it ends, always, with the air smelling of snow and a blue cast to the rock that makes it look as fragile as china. That night we put extra blankets on and fired up the woodstove. The owls were restless; we could hear them in the eaves all night like mice, and I imagined I felt the house shrinking in on itself.

"I want to build one more map," John said after we'd watched the long-bodied semis haul the Dinosaur camp away.

He pulled out his sketches and his notebooks, and I lined up half a dozen of the two-foot-square frames for him to drop his clay into.

"One will do," he said.

He built a range of mountains and then stopped, a peak between his fingers, and looked up at me. "You decide," he said.

"You were going to make Tooth of Time, weren't you?"

"No."

That's what I wanted to see, but not if he didn't want to build it. I thought for a minute. "Horse Thief Gap," I said, "when the scorpions were this small, the dragonflies this large."

He chuckled. "You still want things the way they used to be."

He built a map of our place with an ocean in the middle, with a coastline and a harbor and low hills, and I recognized Horse Thief Gap between two great rocks, but smaller, tucked against the shore. I mixed a glaze for him that's gone unused all these years. It would fire green. If the scale had been larger, I would have put in flowers.

"What happens," I asked, "if we get snow first, and miss all the rains?"

"It's never happened," he said.

"But what if it does?"

"Then maybe Caliope shacks up with Peters."

"Oh, God, imagine that."

"Well, with you, then."

"Oh, God, imagine *that*."

"Or the Hitch."

"Do you mean Caliope with the Hitch, or the Hitch with me?"

"All of you together. Whichever way your fantasies run, Paul."

I stoked the kiln and worked the bellows on the floor. "Did you ever want to be a father, John?"

He didn't answer for a minute. "This is enough for me," he said, and laid a hand on his new map. "How about you?"

"Sure. Once. I thought I could find someone I could build children with."

"Difficult, out here."

"Yes."

"Is it kids or a wife you wanted?" he asked.

"I don't know." It's a man's job to decide what to do with his life, I thought, and a woman's to convince him he's wrong. I swallowed when I realized that's what I'd been doing with John. What had we missed all these years, without that vital energy that stems from dissension? How had we kept our resolve without it?

"You're missing making something, aren't you?"

I nodded.

"You make these," he said, meaning the maps, and I believed him because I had to.

Caliope came up to the house the next day, Saturday, and told us that the Hitch had gone with the Dinosaur Men. "It's lonely down there," she said.

"It gets lonelier tomorrow," I said, "when John leaves. Then there'll be just the two of us around here."

"There's Peters," John said.

"Three of us, then."

"Clay Peters is kind of weird," Caliope said, and suddenly I liked her.

"Weird how?" John asked. I gave him an odd look.

"I don't know." She flipped one palm over, facing up. "It would sound silly."

"Nothing about Peters," I said, "would sound silly."

"How about some lunch?" John asked her. "And a beer."

"Thanks. That's what I came for."

I warmed up the stew I'd made the night before and brought out some bread.

"Someone cooks good," she said. John pointed at me. "I guess," she said, in the middle of eating, "silly or not, he feels evil."

"Why is that silly?" John asked softly.

"It doesn't exist. Evil."

"It doesn't?"

She shook her head. "Not as—you know—a force."

"It takes different shapes," John said.

In his mind, where Peters was concerned, the shape was an absence of life, a diminishment, anyway, of that animation we expect to see in each other, and in all living things. I was startled to remember that I'd seen Peters as womanly. I sat back with a beer in my hand and saw myself with a clarity I'd never attempted—or even desired—before. I'd never set out to be a misogynist, but the things I distrusted were in women.

"Paul?"

I looked up.

"Are you all right?"

I nodded.

"It looks like a gear snapped in there somewhere." He tapped his own temple with a forefinger.

"If you want to go live with Lois, it's all right."

"Gee, thanks, Paul."

I looked at Caliope and saw her for once with all her clothes on. Her eyes flickered between the two of us and settled on me. She was lovely, a bit gaunt, very brown. Her dark hair gleamed. I admired what she'd had to put up with, and was putting up with, in order to build that town of hers in the gully.

"Use the shower up here whenever you want," I told her. "If you get hungry, come on by."

"Thank you."

"I know it's cold down there at night."

"I've got a good bag," she said warily.

"She can have my room while I'm gone," John said. He turned to her. "I'm sorry. You can have my room while I'm gone, Caliope."

"I'll stay with my camera, I think."

"I'll drive you down when it rains," I said.

"I don't think I want to lose that much of my independence."

"All right. You can walk down when it rains."

She laughed. "I'll take you up on the shower," she said. "And one other thing. If you loan me your truck, I can get some things in town."

"I'll drive you in. We need beer."

"That's kind. This is awkward." She blushed a little under her tan. "There's things I want to buy. And I'd like to walk around and look in the windows. And find a place with a bathtub. Maybe rent a room for the night and sleep on a real bed."

"Take the truck," I said. "The keys are in it."

"Not the bright red one," John said.

"The dull red one," I said.

"I won't miss a storm tonight, will I?"

John shook his head.

"Halloween," I said.

She stood up and pulled her hair back over her ears. "How can you know that?"

"Just trust it."

"Well." She turned at the door. "Do you think Peters might need some things?"

"What he needs most—" John and I both said together.

"He can't have," I finished.

She looked at the two of us again, flicking back and forth, and I could read in her mind that we were both weird, too. She held up a hand. "Thanks."

"You could have offered her a bath," John said when the truck started.

"Don't push," I said. And, "Wait a minute."

I ran out. She was having trouble backing with John's pickup parked where it was. "Hold on a second," I told her, and got into John's truck and moved it. "Will you get something for me in town?"

"Sure."

"Beer. And then go to a hardware store and get me a long-handled rake. The best one they've got."

"Okay."

I reached into the glove compartment for my wallet. It had four dollars in it. "Just a minute. I'll get some money from John."

"I've got enough. You can give it to me when I get back. A long-handled rake. Nothing else?"

"Buy something for dinner and I'll cook it."

"Okay. Dinner tomorrow night." She backed nearly to the steps and then drove carefully down the wash.

"What's up?" John asked.

"I've got a date. How much money do you have in that paper bag you brought back from the bank?"

"I don't know. Quite a bit. I spent eighteen for the truck and another couple here and there. Why?"

"You spent another couple thousand here and there?"

"I bought Lois some things."

"Have we got that much money in the bank?"

"Not anymore. We haven't spent anything for thirty years, Paul. That bank's full of our money. Your money; I took mine out. Take yours and it'll fold."

"Buy me a rake."

"What are you going to do with a rake?"

It was better he didn't know. "Maybe it's my wedding present to you," I said. "When you get that house in the suburbs."

"Lois has a rake, and I'm not getting married. How much do you need?"

"Give me a handful of twenties."

He still had the money in the paper bag. He came out of his bedroom with it and fished around for a stack.

"Does Lois let you carry it around like that?"

"She doesn't know I'm rich."

"Why else would she love you?"

"You know," he said, "it's going to be nice to get away from you for a while."

"How long a while, John?"

He gave me a sheaf of bills and wrote down a number on the bank receipt he was still carrying. He sat down, tucking the bag between a leg and a stump. "Seriously?"

"Seriously."

"At least a month. Probably two. Unless Lois throws me out, and she might. Look for me at Christmas."

"She'll want to keep you for Christmas. Decorating the tree. Presents with big red bows. All the kids—and the kids' kids—around, and turkey dinner."

"Maybe."

"No maybe. Holidays are made for women."

"After Christmas, then."

"That's New Year's."

"After New Year's."

"Valentine's Day."

He grinned at me.

"They've got the calendar rigged, John."

"Well, then, tomorrow will be good-bye forever."

We set up the chessboard and played most of the night, and I lost a hundred and ten dollars cash. He gave me change from his own stack of twenties he'd given me. The next day around noon he packed his gear and threw it and the bag of money on the front seat and drove off.

"I left a receipt for the truck on the table," he told me. "Send it to the Foundation for me. And if you feel like it, add up the guesses in our logs and send those, too."

"Let's just wait until Arlyle gets here. But he won't pay them."

"I don't know about that, Paul. It's the only real research we've ever done."

I took his hand and shook it. Held it, really.

"You know where to find me, Paul."

"I'll let you find me," I said.

He drove off, and I watched his new red truck cross the desert and pass my old red one, coming back.

13

"Rake," she said when she got out of the pickup. She lifted it out of the bed and showed me. She looked at the rock and sand around the place and left it leaning against the tailgate. "And dinner." She lifted out a bag.

"What am I making?"

"I'm making."

"Have you ever cooked on a woodstove?"

She shook her head.

"Let me do the making. What is it?"

"Spaghetti."

"No fooling?"

"What did you have in mind? Here." She handed me the bag and I looked in.

I pawed through it. "I don't know. Lamb chops, maybe. Fish. Turkey. Roast. A big ham. Porterhouse steaks."

"Spaghetti is my specialty," she said. "I bought salad fixings, good bread, fresh butter, and dessert. It cost you a bundle, so you'd better enjoy it."

"What do I owe you?"

"Including the rake?"

"Yes."

"Thirty-nine dollars."

I gave her two of John's twenties and took the food into the kitchen.

"That wine's hot," she said. "It was in the sun all the way back."

"I'll put it on the veranda." I set the two bottles out in the shade.

She'd bought some clothes in town, too, and I thought—mending my ways as I was—that I should say something. "Nice clothes," I said, and bit my lip, rusty.

"Oh. Thanks."

She had on cream-colored slacks with a high, tight waist and black, low-heeled slipperlike shoes, and a short-sleeved black blouse that was gathered in nicely at the neck. She was a nicely built, beautiful girl, and she had every reason to feel pretty. I turned away and began pulling things from the sack.

"Let me do it." She bumped me away with a hip. "You get the stove cooking and you can tell me if I do something clumsy, but this is my sauce to make."

She cut up tomatoes and peppers and vegetables I hadn't seen in years and began slicing up a package of stewing beef.

"Stewing beef in spaghetti?"

"You wait."

She'd bought a dozen little red-and-white cans of spices. "I didn't know what you had," she said. She laid out all her prizes on the table. "I passed Mr. Suope on the way out," she said.

"It's John. I'm Paul."

"Cal," she said, and turned, bowed formally, and held out her hand.

"I'm more comfortable with Caliope," I said, and shook it. "How'd you get that name?"

She shrugged. "Parents. There isn't any sort of cute story that goes with it, though I've made up a few."

"Thanks for being so forgiving."

She looked over her shoulder, and I thought she would say something, but she turned back again without speaking. "It must be hard," she said finally, "to share your front yard with strangers. Even a front yard as big as this one."

"Like I said, thanks for being so forgiving."

"I don't really understand," she said. "I'm faking it, a bit. I grew up in an apartment house in a block of apartment houses, in a city of apartment houses, so I'm only guessing." She kept her back to me, cutting. "And I confess that I haven't treated you all that well, either."

"How's that?"

"I wasn't always dressing for the heat," she said quietly. "And I knew you were watching when I took my dips in the lake."

"It's a vengeance I can live with," I said.

"Still. It wasn't nice."

Oh, yes it was, I wanted to say. "I'm sorry we looked."

"Don't be. It was my doing, more than yours. This place—"

"I know. It changes you."

"No, not that." She turned around with the knife in her fist. Light gleamed along its blade. "It makes you unafraid."

"Not me."

She laughed. "What are you afraid of?"

I sat down at the table and rolled a tomato between my hands. When I didn't answer right away she turned back to her work.

"Sorry," she said.

"No need to be. I'm just adding up all the things I'm afraid of and trying to put them into some sort of order."

"Right."

"Everything about this place scares me, but the outside scares me even more."

"Right," she said again, more firmly, giving me the opening to make it into a joke if I wanted.

"The important thing about cooking on a woodstove," I said, "is that anything you touch will burn. Those pot holders hanging on the wall aren't decoration."

"Got it."

"Simmer is difficult."

"When I'm ready for simmer, I'll let you know," she said.

"Keep things moving or they'll stick."

"I always do."

I watched her bottom move in the cream-colored slacks as if in corroboration. "I'll be in the other room," I said, getting up. "Holler if you need me."

"I will."

I could have had a daughter her age. I could have had one older. I'd done my college work thirty years ago. I took a beer out onto the porch and walked along the length of the veranda, standing up on my toes to look in on the elf owls, but they were huddled down, asleep, and didn't look back. I ran my hand for some reason along the wall and looked at the whitewash that came away on my palm, as fine and dry as chalkdust. All I needed, I thought, was a cave wall to press it against.

She cooked and served dinner without any help from me. It was one of the best meals ever. She even made the salad dressing, a creamy white ranch with a bite. She poured the wine into the clay cups John had made years ago. It tasted sticky; it might have been the wine—I can't remember when I'd last had some—or it might have been the New Mexico heat baked into it, but it was probably the cups.

For the first few hours I was on my guard not to do something stupid, not to say anything that could be considered an advance or clumsy lechery, but toward evening I grew more comfortable sitting with her. Most of that was her doing: she was as relaxed as if she belonged here. I cleaned up the dishes and then joined her in the chairs on the porch.

"I dropped some things off at the tent before I came up," she said. "A bottle of champagne among them."

"The heat will kill it."

"That's what I was just thinking. Can I put it in your fridge?"

"Sure."

"It's for when I get my flood."

"You deserve it."

"You think?"

I had to sort out whether or not that was coy, and I decided it wasn't. Her idea of coy, after all, was nakedness. "I think," I said, "that I've never met anybody with so much desire to make this"—I tapped my temple—"real. Whatever your work is, you're not afraid to do it."

"Do you want to know what my work is?"

"Will I understand it?"

"Sure."

"Okay, then."

She settled into the chair and tipped it back, as John does, balancing by the pressure of her foot against the rail. She looked better doing it, though, than John.

"It might sound silly," she said.

"Try."

"I know it'll sound idealistic."

"There's nothing wrong with that."

"All right." She took a deep breath and I smelled the wine. "I started out wanting to film hurricanes. Not just hurricanes but earthquakes and volcanoes and meteor strikes. But they don't come along all that often, except for volcanoes, and somebody has just done an unbeatable film on them."

"Really?"

"Kilauea, in Hawaii. Beautiful stuff. Anyway, we're so busy burning holes in the atmosphere and ripping up forests that I thought I'd try to turn things around a little and film the raw—" She stopped, looking for a better word than force. "The raw—"

"Elemental," I suggested.

"Yes. The elemental. That's the idealism part," she said. "And maybe the silly part, too. But that's not what my dissertation is about."

I waited for her to gather all this together.

"I guess the simplest way to say it is that film—and the tricks you can play with it—can be powerful all on its own. It's not just the flood I want to film; I want to make it my flood, with my eye and my camera."

"I see," I said.

"No, I've said it all wrong. There's a music in it," she said, "without sound. Does that make sense?"

I thought of the caves, and the pools, and thought it did.

"There's a dance in a storm," she said. "A dance in a hurricane. A—production, for want of a better word—in catastrophe."

"Collisions," I said, thinking out loud.

"Exactly." She sat up, planting the chair's legs, and stared at me very seriously. "It still sounds stupid, the way I've said it," she said. "I've only been given one real language to explain myself, and that's the camera."

"You're lucky," I said. "Some of us haven't been given any language at all." I thought of John and his marvelous hands. I've always been more than a little jealous of his ability to re-create in the round any form he wished.

We sat for a while longer, but both of us knew that the conversation had played out. If she'd asked me about my work, I wouldn't have done as well as she had explaining it. That, too, had required a courage I lacked.

"Will you drop me off," she said, waving a hand at the basin, "and bring back my champagne?"

"In a minute. I want to show you something." The minute stretched into fifteen, but she sat there, not talking, until the desert and the sky were the same deep perfect blue. "There. As far as I know, you can't see that down below."

"No," she said. "No, you can't. You do understand, then, the language I've been talking about."

I nodded.

"Would you mind very much if I brought my stuff up here tomorrow evening and shot it?"

"As long as you don't tell anybody where you did it," I said. "I don't want a desert full of color hunters next spring."

She bobbed her head like a child and then thanked me for dinner.

"You can thank me for dinner any time you want to come up here and sweat all afternoon over a hot stove. It was entirely my pleasure."

"Is John coming back soon?" she asked as we were in the truck and heading down.

"Not until Christmas."

"You can visit me, too," she said, "if you want to sit knee to knee in my living room."

I took her down to her tent. There was a pinprick of light in the distance. Peters's room. It didn't belong in the desert, and I told her so.

"It's comforting, really," she said. "It's on sometimes until dawn. A nightlight."

"There's nothing in this desert to hurt you," I said.

"Snakes and scorpions."

"Well, yes, but other than that."

"No lions or tigers or bears, you mean."

"Right. No lions or tigers or bears." Or sex-starved, old-man maniacs. "Just snakes and scorpions and gila monsters."

"Do you have *those* around here?"

"I haven't seen any in years."

"Wonderful."

"Put a board across those seats in the blind and sleep high, and sleep peacefully."

"I might do that," she said.

"Sleep in John's room," I said, "anytime you want."

"I'll think about it."

"I'm no danger to you either."

"If you say so," she said.

"Good night."

The house was twice empty when I got back to it. I noticed now a perfume she must have been wearing that I hadn't smelled. I followed it from room to room and found it strongest in the doorway to the kitchen, and like a lovesick kid I leaned against the jamb and breathed it in. I wanted to lick it. I put her champagne in the refrigerator. I saw her again as she had stood in the kitchen cutting up vegetables, in her cream-colored slacks and black slippers and the blouse bunched at her neck, but didn't undress her. Instead I found myself thinking about hurricanes and diving through the wall cloud, taking pictures.

She came back the next evening as she'd promised, bringing her camera and tripod. She set it up in front of the steps and gratefully took the beer I offered her.

"This is good equipment," she said, "but I don't know if I'll get the full effect of that blue light."

"I think it takes all outdoors to do that," I said. "But it's worth a try."

We waited without having anything else to say. I told her when it was time, and she ran down the steps and turned the camera on. It seemed to me that it lasted half a minute longer than usual but that was probably my imagination. It goes three minutes by my watch; I've timed it more than a few times.

"Have you eaten?" I asked her.

"A sandwich. This afternoon."

So I made dinner this time, and she seemed to enjoy it every bit as much as she had her own cooking.

Out on the porch, under the moon, she told me a little bit about herself. Growing up in the city had been a whirlwind, with none of the lazy Sundays or baseball games I remembered from my small town. I sidestepped a few questions about childhood, feeling awkward in the kind of conversation we make in beginnings.

"It's so long ago now," I said, "it's a different person."

"How about John, then? Where's he from?"

I had to think. "He's a farmboy. From Kansas or someplace."

"How'd you meet?"

"In the war." I saved us both the gory spots and told her, instead, a simple story about acquaintances who become friends.

When she wanted to know why we'd come to New Mexico, I had to stop and think again. Why had we?

"Different reasons for each of us, I think," I said slowly. "I was wondering about that not too long ago, remembering how we'd made the decision, but that part's lost. All I can remember is that we made it."

She didn't say anything.

"John didn't want to come, I remember that. And I did want to come, but I don't know why."

Now she nodded.

"Maybe the better question," I said, "is why we haven't left."

"The answer to that's easy," she said.

"Tell me then."

"It's your home. And your work."

"I don't know what my work is."

"Of course you do."

I drove her home that night, and the next night, and then she agreed to move into John's room if she wouldn't be in the way.

"I leave the keys in the pickup," I said. "You can go anytime you want, day or night."

I think that made her easier about it. In a very short time I came to look forward to mornings, when she would be up before me and sitting at the table in the kitchen with a cup of fresh coffee and that soft yellow New Mexico sunlight dancing on her hands.

She asked to take over the cooking chores, but I wouldn't let her. I like it. We threw pots on John's wheel, and as I began teaching her, I realized how much I already knew. My cups and plates looked like cups and plates, while all of hers, even a vase she tried, looked like ashtrays. She took a shower every night and asked if she was using all the water. She was using half of it because I got into the same practice. You don't smell your own scent until there's another in the house. John and I, I guess, smell the same. We settled into a comfortable familiarity that was moving toward friendship and I wanted to pick up the phone we don't have and call John and tell him he didn't deserve any medals for living with me all these years; other people could do it, too.

And then a day dawned with rain and I looked at my calendar watch. The thirty-first. Halloween, and Jamieson's storm.

It rained harder, and then harder still, until by noon there was hail bouncing off the steps and the pickup. Caliope was anxious to get back, so I drove her to the blind. The rain I'd wanted for months I now wanted to stop, but it was coming in off the Pacific and stacking clouds up like airplanes over Logan; it had come all those thousands of miles to make lightning over New Mexico, and my wishes weren't going to stop it.

I sat in the truck by the blind for an hour and then shouted at her to fire up her generator and get the lights going, and then I drove up to the house to watch the show from my porch. I couldn't see her place from there—I'd have to climb Rayado to do that—but I watched the wash out front begin to run in streams.

There isn't more lightning anywhere in the world than New Mexico. The storm intensified as night came on, and for a long time I watched my world through the blue flickering, saw the desert etched by it as the rain fell in sheets and curtains and finally in a roar of hail and rain that banged down so hard I could hear it drumming on the dirt and the hollowness the earth has underneath it.

I sat in my chair, in my jacket, in the middle of the storm. A flutter caught my eye and I turned to see, at the corner of the house, one of the adult elf owls strutting back and forth on the boards, his head bobbing, his neck feathers ruffled against the wind and rain. He opened his beak to squawk—it's a plaintive sound: a *gheek!* but I could-n't hear it in that noise—and he stared at me with those huge golden eyes, and I imagined him asking me to stop it. He marched across the veranda and took up a watch sta-tion under my chair and from time to time would reach up to peck at the fraying canvas straps that hold the thing to-gether. I would have reached down to soothe him but for that honed, hooked beak.

The wash was running freely now, tumbling small stones down it, and I knew without any doubt that this was Caliope's flood. I wouldn't be able to drive down the wash to see her; she wouldn't be able to walk up it to see me. Ex-cept for the owl under my chair and his family in the eaves, I was as alone as I'd ever been. It wasn't possible to see more than thirty feet, and at times even the pickup—barely half that from me—disappeared completely in the downpour.

I knew as certainly as I've known anything that my tree was lost; that the tunnel would wash out from underneath it and the great old thing would topple. Peters would have his excavation begun for him, as he'd no doubt planned.

Elemental, I thought, and elementary. Why did everybody else use the land and the weather, while the weather and the land used us? John and I had missed an essential education.

I got up to go inside and make some coffee and the owl hopped sideways out from under the chair and screamed at me silently and then—half hopping, half flying—made his way back around the corner and back up under the eaves.

The storm stopped at two o'clock. It didn't slow down, muttering, as storms usually do, but simply quit. I waited, sleepy, for it to begin again, guessing I was in its eye, but it was over. I slept in those small dark hours with lightning still flashing on the insides of my eyelids, the long-delayed afterimages, or the colors that we see when sleeping. The morning was crisp and clear and cold, the red rock gleaming, the sky the color you find inside the shells of eggs, with just a hint of blue.

I made another pot of coffee and a breakfast of eggs and bacon, and as I finished it Caliope stumbled up the slope to the house, muddy, soaked, happy.

"Destruction does something for you," I said at the door. "How did it go?"

"It was beautiful," she said. "It was astonishing. Everything I'd hoped."

"Coffee?"

"Please."

"Breakfast?"

"I couldn't eat." Her face glowed like the rock, as if it had been scrubbed with wire brushes. "On the other hand, I could eat anything. Everything."

"How'd you get up here?"

"On my hands and knees."

"Champagne with breakfast?"

She shook her head. "After." She followed me into the kitchen to stand by the stove. "I'd shower," she said, "but I'm too cold."

"How about a hot bath?"

"Don't joke with me. I'd kill old people right now for a hot bath."

"I'm not joking. There's a place."

She looked at me for a long minute, weighing the dangers, perhaps, or guessing if I was lying or not, and then she said, "Bring the champagne and let's go."

"It might be a wild ride," I said, thinking of the wash and the new desert floor.

"A small risk."

"It's not your truck." But I took the bottle I'd stashed for her and we climbed into the pickup.

We slid down, as I'd feared, but luckily it's a straight enough drop that not steering was a minor inconvenience. I'd never get up it again, though, until it had a chance to drain. There was more water than road under the wheels.

I took the rake and the lantern into the caves and stopped at the opening to speak to her.

"Do you mind darkness and rats?"

"Love 'em." She looked at the rake. "Unless that's why you have that, in which case I could be talked out of it."

"Come on."

I held the light out so she could see, so I stumbled a couple of times, but I knew the path well enough to get to the pools without much trouble, and when she was next to one she put her hands out over it as if warming them at a fire.

"Hot tubs," she said.

"What's that?"

"Home."

I put the lantern down and expected her to jump in with her clothes on, imagining the cloudy water close around her as her jeans gave up their dirt, but she peeled them off and left them in a wet wad and slid into the pool. "Well, come on in," she said.

I dropped her clothes into the next pool—the hell with it—and took mine off with my back to her, and then, embarrassed as an old man ought to be, got in with her.

She put a warm wet hand on either side of my face and kissed me, as a lover might, I suppose, or a friend, or a wife, but with such a simple and uncomplicated generosity that I was left shaken. It was better than sex, which I didn't get.

I lowered the rake into the sulphur pool before we left and dragged up a mess of pitted bone. A yellow, gummy sheath had begun to form around them and the bone-ends were dimpled, as if by acid.

"What's that?" she asked, and then covered her mouth, understanding.

"It's what Peters is after," I said. "But he'll never get them."

"It's a shame she ended up here," she said.

"Yes." I'd intended to rake them out and haul them up to Tooth of Time, but now that I'd seen them I decided to leave them be. I wish I'd never looked.

I took Caliope out of the caves and back to the house and, the next day, into town.

"I'll mail you a copy of this"—she held up a flat black plastic box that was her flood—"if you give me an address."

"General delivery, Raton. And give me instructions on how to play it."

"Just plug it into a VCR."

"You see, I wouldn't have known that."

I held her hand while we waited for the bus, and I felt foolish doing it, fatherly, and she was uncomfortable, too, I think, but didn't pull away. I watched as the driver stored her gear between the wheels and then I leaned forward and gave her a peck, as you do with relatives, and then as the bus drove off I stood there and waved, as I have while watching UFOs.

14

What was I to her or she to me? I don't know. There are parts of me, now, that I don't recognize. I'd been wrong about everything except the monkey puzzle.

It had probably leaned over drunkenly for a time before its own weight ripped its roots up, and it may have lain cockeyed before sliding down Kit Carson Mesa. It had died at the bottom of the slope, its bark already whitening. I wish Caliope had filmed that instead of her flood.

I walked along the creekbed, picking two-by-fours from the mud and throwing them up on the bank to load, later, into the truck. Most of her town floated on Miami Lake, buoyed by the salt. Brightly painted plywood squares and window frames bobbed about, the aftermath of a cheap cruise ship being torpedoed.

The cleanup took me two weeks. The plywood was nearly useless, but I hauled it back anyway, sheet by sheet, and stacked it in tall, warped piles to dry. I left the two-by-fours in a wet heap to be sawed. I'd use what I could to build map crates, and the rest I'd break apart for stove-wood. I made a note to myself to haul in alder for the winter. We need to begin collecting huge stacks of it—a dozen cords or so—about this time.

Peters started working the cut where the monkey puzzle had been. I've seen him up there even in the driving rain, a shapeless, yellow, rain-slicked thing, and I wonder if he'll draw lightning, as I do. Twice I've seen him crossing the desert with his pack on his shoulders, having dragged—or dredged—who knows what from the top of that mesa. Now the snow's begun and even he has had to stop.

I dreamed that Peters's small house caught fire and that he rushed out onto the snow with his few possessions and that I, after wrestling with myself for an hour or two (watching with binoculars as he stamped in the snow and slowly froze), invited him to come and live with me. He took over the shed, setting a table on top of the crash piece, and we sat there side by side morning and afternoon making maps of the things we knew.

I drove down every few days after that dream and watched his house through the binoculars. The vented smoke from his stove swirled in the wind and obscured the outlines of his small place as if a deliberate hand were hiding it. Heaps of wood, covered with tarpaulins, lay in mounds around the place, as dirt and gravel is dumped by trucks at a constructions site; he must have made arrangements with somebody in town, and they must deliver at night. He'd need, too, without a truck of any sort, to have planned deliveries of food and water and kerosene for his lamp. Who could live like that?

By the first week of December I almost convinced myself that he had died and the stove was somehow consuming itself or the inside of his shack, or that I was caught in a single white moment that never changed: the smoke that hung around his place in a haze was last week's smoke that had never dissipated, and in April I would find him as he'd been in November, that white spiral of bone I'd predicted.

His death weighed on me, so I went down and knocked at his door, shivering. He took a long time answering. The window was frosted with heat and I put my hand against it. Plastic.

I heard a chair scrape. He opened the door and stared at me for a minute, then opened it wider, and I went in. He'd grown a short white beard and lost weight and except for those lifeless eyes could be my brother, or me. There was a cot in one corner with a blue wool blanket on it. A small, simple wooden desk and crude chair he'd knocked together took up the other corner. A lantern hung from the ceiling. He had several crates of canned food, a cookstove, a woodstove and a box of wood, and a large galvanized washtub for dishes and clothes and a bath. There was a tablet of paper on his desk, two pencils, and a pair of reading glasses. It's where he worked on his archaeology. I have a place like that—the kitchen table—where I struggle with this, my own work; this accounting; this archaeology of myself. John told me that there's always a reckoning and a settling of debt.

"How are you getting along?" I asked.

"All right," he said. He sat in the chair and motioned me over to the cot. I thought I detected an accent in those two words I hadn't noticed before—German, or something like it; Russian, perhaps—but maybe it was the heat that had thickened his voice.

He waited patiently, blinking in that heat as regularly as if he had a metronome working in his brain.

The cot trembled under me. I was afraid to move, sure that it would collapse and bury me in dirty bedclothes that smelled of Peters.

"It's damned cold out," I said. "I was worried." I pulled my jacket open and spread the two halves. "I guess I needn't be."

"No," Peters said. "It's fine in here."

Sam McGee, frozen in the North and cremated by his poet-narrator, says the same from the furnace.

"Food? Water? Wood? Everything okay?"

"Everything's fine," Peters said.

Loneliness! I wanted to shout. Don't you go crazy in an eight-by-eight box? Don't you want to scream when you hear a snowflake land on your roof like a rock? Are you so lifeless that you can stand yourself every minute of every day? "I'll be going, then," I said.

"I'd like to borrow that shoulder bone I gave you," he said as if he hadn't heard me.

"I'll bring it by."

"Do you want to see something?" he said shyly, as if he were about to unzip his pants and pull out something monstrous, or go to the cupboard he didn't have and open it on a shelf of still dripping heads. The archaeology crew. Arlyle.

"Sure."

"Excuse me." He reached between my legs before I could move and pulled a box from under the cot. He lifted out a large square of paper and unfolded it; he unfolded it again and again until he could barely hold it, and then he tacked it up on the wall with four oversized thumbtacks. "A map of what we've done," he said. "I thought it might interest you."

The desert was drawn in exquisite detail. Even some of Jamieson's webs were inked in, and he must have had a helicopter, I thought, to get those complicated patterns right. I looked for our place—to see what it looked like to him—but only the edges of Rayado were there, and all of Gonzalitos' eastern face, but not Horse Thief Gap. The orientation was odd; upright, southwest was at the top instead of north.

"Is that what you're doing here?" I asked. "Making maps?"

He nodded. "It'll take months. All winter. This is the entire site. It's graphed, as you can see"—I looked closer and saw fine penciled squares—"and numbered, and I've begun on the larger-scale maps, each square there"—he tapped the sheet-sized map—"this size," and tapped it again.

"What are the red dots?" The map had a pox.

"Excavations."

Two at Gonzalitos. One in the center of Kit Carson, my monkey puzzle. Three dozen others scattered at random around the desert floor.

"We pulled it all up in such a hurry," he said, "and left so much more behind that I'm turning our field notes into the maps we should have made then."

"Why did you do it that way, if it wasn't the right way?"

"That's what they wanted."

"Arlyle?"

"The Foundation. They wanted all the bones we could get, and they wanted them fast. Sometimes they care nothing for science."

"Can I see one of the larger ones?"

He pulled another map from the box and again unfolded it until he could barely hold it, and pinned it up. This time the desert's lines were faint, but the bones buried in it were drawn with bold dark strokes of ink, each with its number beside it. They lay jumbled on top of each other, scattered by the random hands of weather and water and time, and a few, here and there, were shaded in completely in the dark ink.

"Why's that?"

"Those are still in the ground," he said. "We'll pull them out in the spring."

"We?"

He smiled. "Maybe me."

"I didn't think you had time to gather all this," I said.

"We're all mapmakers," he said. "The whole crew." You, too. "I have all their notebooks, and all this time."

"But each bone." I studied the huge map and was overwhelmed. The shapes lay on the page like cells under a microscope, their hidden geometry apparent, discovered.

"And each fragment," Peters said.

"It's amazing." I meant it.

Peters looked at me without expression. "It's hard work."

I left him, unsettled by it all. In one winter he would map the desert in more convincing detail than John and I have done in our lifetimes. We knew its elevations and its distance, but that lump of human coal Peters knew its secrets.

I began in the shed to build and model in clay. I'd watched John long enough to know how to go about it. My fingers possessed a speed and surety that surprised me, as if they'd been waiting all these years to show me their knowledge. It took me only a week to begin coaxing real figures from the clay, and that, I figured, was the time it took the brain to learn which muscles to route its messages to. Soon my hands were pulling up recognizable forms.

I worked a fair likeness of John, afraid that if I didn't I would forget what he looked like. I built Peters and got him right. Then Caliope. My God, what a thrill it was to take the picture in my mind and make it actual. It astonished me—it astonishes me still—that talent can lie hidden like dinosaur bones all this time. I built a zoo of long-dead animals, grotesqueries and gargoyles, and stood them in the empty map shelves after firing prehistoric colors into their hides.

And—not to compete with John but to make this place my own—I've begun a sculpture like the crash piece, with that diplodocus shoulder bone at its center. I'm going to dig up that plumb bob and hang it from the ceiling so that it's aimed straight at that smooth hole.

The first of this week I received a package from Caliope. Almost Christmas. I'd brought the instrument into town, finally, to have it recalibrated. I spun the strange flat box she'd sent me in my hands for a minute and then took it to a store that sells televisions and stereos and gadgets of that sort, and I set it down on the counter and said, "I've got this, and I want to see what's on it."

"What's on it?" He gave me a wink and a sort of leer, but after I stared at him for a few seconds he got businesslike again and said he could rent me a VCR for a good price.

"How much?"

"With a two hundred dollar deposit—refundable, of course—I rent it for ten dollars a day."

"That's all I need?"

"That's all. Just plug it into the wall, and this into the TV"—he was holding up two thin cables—"and switch your set to channel three."

"I don't have a set," I said.

"No TV?"

"No TV."

"Well, that's no problem. I rent those, too."

"Well," I said, rubbing my beard, "I don't have any electricity either." I have a little, but I save it for keeping the beer cold.

The gadget man looked at me as if I wasn't from this planet.

"Can we set it up here in the store?" I asked. "I'll pay the rental, and for your time."

"There's nothing dirty on there, is there?"

I told him I didn't think so. I said it would probably only run for a minute or two. "I just need a chair to sit in."

He lifted a TV up on the counter and hooked up the VCR and turned the whole superstructure away from the showroom so I'd have some privacy if a customer came in (none did), and then he stood back against the wall, out of the way, and watched with me. The snow on the screen cleared to a sharp picture of Caliope's flood. If she'd had a million dollars and a good sound stage, she couldn't have gotten better results.

There was a black screen, and then a blue jagged sword of lightning, black again, with a roll of thunder on that black screen, and the sound of rain. The camera found a flat rock under the glare of her lights, and the rain bounced off it. Each drop was impaled with light. We heard thunder again and the rain thrumming down at the same steady rate. Perhaps she'd done that in the laboratory—making the rain louder than it had been—but perhaps not.

From the rain bouncing on the rock, the camera moved back until an edge of town could be seen, crosslit by the lights on each side of the ravine that gave, oddly, a slightly orange cast to everything. The creekbed puddled and grew muddy and as we watched began to run with water.

The lightning cracked so loudly once that I heard her say, "Oh, God," and I wondered, briefly, why she'd left that on the tape, but then agreed as she must have that it was right. The camera, rooted as it was, had only the zoom to work with, and she'd used it well, moving back up the creekbed, through the town, a walking eye.

Then she focused on one building after another, a series of still photographs. Even in the rain the detail was sharp enough under those lights to see nail heads. Each shot ended in a blur, and when the clarity had been reestablished there was another storefront: hotel, jail, the church I had helped Peters build.

She held the camera on the church and diminished the storm's volume; behind it a rumble was building that wasn't thunder—I've heard it before, terrifying: flood.

It looked like dry earth moving as it hit the town. Rocks in a brown charging cliff swallowed the first two buildings and pushed the rest before it. The gadget man let his breath out, and I realized I'd been holding mine as well.

The town swept past, sticks rising up at weird angles, and then the creekbed was dancing with brown water that cleared, slowly, and took on the sheen of oil. The lights in their aluminum scaffolding were clearly reflected on its surface. The flood was past; Caliope's town was gone.

The screen went black and I reached up to turn it off, but the gadget man put his hand on my arm. "No noise," he said, and I was about to ask him what that meant when the TV lit up again, and we saw the same sequence of events, shot for shot, in slow motion. The lightning, frozen that way, burned its image on my eyes, and the brown surge of flood was as close as I care to come to seeing God.

When it was over, a single credit glimmered on the dark screen. *Flood: Caliope Jones.*

It is mine to keep forever, and I might buy a TV and a VCR to watch it again on dark, equinoctial nights.

I paid the man and collected the tape and left. When I think how I gathered up the aftermath of that—stick by stick to burn in my stove—I wish I hadn't.

I picked up the instrument before noon. "Way off," the man said. I took it home and shot a monument and got it right. Now when John and I lie—if we ever do this again—we'll be lying on purpose. The man who recalibrated the instrument had tied another plumb bob on without asking. I'll leave it, for now, if for no other reason than to remind me (I shouldn't need the reminder after all this time) not to take hold of sun-hot brass.

I carry its triangular imprint on my palm.

Peters's little house burned down on Christmas. I found him on the porch cradling an armload of maps, looking like a schoolboy waiting for the bus.

I've put him in the shed, which is all he asked. Sitting at the kitchen table, getting all this down, I think of him tucked away in there, and I look in on him from time to time (hell, I stand over him) and watch him draw his maps, and that bare one-hundred-watt bulb throws my shadow over his. We never needed to steal those bones; all we needed to steal were the notebooks.

I'm afraid Peters and I, not John and I, will spend the rest of our lives together. Although I no longer believe in conspiracies, I know there's a purpose in my being and my passing. We have the same job; I am connected to John and Arlyle and to you all by invisible strings.

The night Wilkens shot down that flying saucer all those years ago, and we came home with that one small piece, John asked me what I wanted most in the next life.

I invented a philosophy on the spot, as you do sometimes. "I guess what I'd like most," I'd said, "is to be watching in a million years or so when the next species"—*you, maybe*—"mines my bones, breaking into the earth with tiny hammers."

Tonight on my way to the shed to check on Peters and his work, I looked in on the elf owls and saw staring back at me huge, half-lidded, sleepy eyes. It must be much the way God has watched us all this time, as I've mapped his contours in my notebook, and John has reconstructed his face.

LaPorte County Public Library
LaPorte, Indiana

GAYLORD S